RICHARD'S BURDEN

by S. Thomas

DORRANCE
PUBLISHING CO
EST. 1920
PITTSBURGH, PENNSYLVANIA 15238

The contents of this work, including, but not limited to, the accuracy of events, people, and places depicted; opinions expressed; permission to use previously published materials included; and any advice given or actions advocated are solely the responsibility of the author, who assumes all liability for said work and indemnifies the publisher against any claims stemming from publication of the work.

Dorrance Publishing Co
585 Alpha Drive
Pittsburgh, PA 15238
Visit our website at *www.dorrancebookstore.com*

ISBN: 978-1-6470-2470-3
eISBN: 978-1-6470-2930-2

After all this time, it seemed like we had spent every day like this. Huddled together, whole. We were just waiting for time to pass. But our patience was running out, and time had no agenda.

FOREWORD

There was a wooden shed just beyond a creek on the outskirts of my home-town. It didn't seem to belong to anyone. I passed it every day going to and from school in my beamer. It was old and worn from the brutality of the elements. Some of the wood was warped and split beyond repair. I knew every-thing about how it looked; its shape, its color, even its shadow. It was *just* in the back of my mind. But if you had asked me, I would have told you that I didn't know. I would have told you that it didn't matter. It was insignificant—not even worth talking about. As was she—insignificant. Every scar, every blemish—not even worth asking about. They were just a part of her, and she was just a part of the scenery. Always in the back. But in only two months, her trials would become my own.

WEEK 1

CHAPTER ONE

I don't know what makes us different, do you? Aside from the DNA and physical features. Everyone has their own fingerprint, but do we differ in thought, and desire, and reason? Who tells us we're different, or why some are chosen over others? After a certain point, I suppose you think you've met them all. The shy one, the outgoing one, the sly one, the silly one. I'm the chameleon. As soon as you think you see me—understand me, you're mistaken. I transform right before your eyes. I trick you into seeing day in the nighttime. It's a sleight of hand. A game I play where I show you what you want to see. You look where I tell you to look, and while you're distracted, I get to understand who you are. I know you better than you know yourself, and I'm damn impressed with myself for it. More importantly, I know what you want to see. And I'll use it to my advantage.

Back to you. After a certain point, to you every place starts to seem the same. They breed the same people. They evoke the same emotions. They look the same as every other place you've been. Then, when you think you know everything because everyone and every place seems the same your mind stops. You stop learning. You shut out new ideas and information, and you teach your kids the same thing you were taught, the same things you learned. Because you know everyone, every place, and everything, right? There is nothing new to teach them. You let them become who they are with your beliefs learned as law.

The place my parents sent me to gain an education taught me so much more than they intended; so much more than I think they cared to learn themselves. I would consider my parents wealthy, as would most of the world. To put it blatantly, looking at our finances, we gained an excess of 25,000 dollars a month after bills were covered. What my mother didn't drain on alcohol and parties, and my father didn't throw into risky investments and trips with liabilities, they spent on my matriculation.

My high school was a private school, with the option to board. I lived fifteen minutes away. I did board my first two years, then earned my freedom to stay at home regardless of whether or not my parents were present. Many students were from in-state. Most were from more southern places. They enjoyed the luxuries of old money. Old money, and old values. We had all of the makings of a place you would want to send your child to. Uniform adhering to the demands of the future workplace—button-up shirt, tie, and slacks for men; the business equivalent for women. Stellar teachers and lesson plans, the kind that aroused college admissions teams. Oh, and the facilities! Each dedicated to and named after a generous donor. Each one built more and more grandiose than the former. We got the prospects on the tour every time. It was never a question of "Do you want to attend?" But rather, "Are you eligible to attend?"

But the inside. Inside the facilities, inside the students. Every place has its spiders hidden in the walls and you won't know until you move in and they start to crawl out and they crawl all over you. Antiquated notions that no one dared correct and the cobwebs no one dared touch. We led structured lives, which included the culture. Don't stray from the structure and you will survive—as a student in the classroom and in the halls.

How I grew up, I learned to listen before I acted. And then I acted. I did what I needed to survive. I thought I needed to survive; I couldn't see past it. And I was exhausted. People came in and out of my life and I placed no significance on them but made sure they didn't see me. Didn't see the spiders that lay in wait, the cobwebs that laced my mind.

I heard those spiders and the song they played in my ear. And I sang along.

I heard a tiny ticking sound, the metronome melody.

People kept coming in and out of my vision, looming over me like they were swimming in water effortlessly above me. A man's voice was fading in and out. Shh . . . . I listened to the tiny ticking sound. I loved it. It was so slight and insignificant, but it kept ticking. It kept persevering, though most of the time no one paid attention to it. The voice was finally starting to fade out again when I felt a sharp pain on my right side just below my shoulder blade. I jumped and my eyes shot wide open. In front of my face was a piece of paper with numbered math questions on it. Around me there were other students also sitting in desks, all staring at me—except for one girl of course; she was staring out the window. Just beyond the piece of paper, I realized my teacher was standing in front of my desk, glaring at me. I sighed. I fell asleep again in Math, woken again by Richard who sat beside me. I looked over at him and gave him a thumbs-up. He responded with a nod and two thumbs up. He pointed to the teacher and whispered, "I don't think he noticed." I smiled. Teacher sighed and told me to try to stay awake. I nodded. The bell rang and class was over. All the students, including me, packed up their bags. Richard was out of the room before the bell had even finished resonating. I wanted to leave too, but the teacher was still standing in front of my desk.

"Yes?" I inquired.

He started to talk to me about staying awake and doing work and other things at a reasonable time and the dangers of procrastination and what not. He droned on and on despite my apparent lack of concern, and growing anxiety to leave. I nodded and apologized fervently. The conversation was finally over and I escaped out of the room.

That was my last class of the day, and it was Wednesday so that meant I had to go to an activities committee meeting. I actually hated being on the committee; it was so time consuming. I joined solely because it was popular and people expected me to be on it. But we were planning prom for the next couple of weeks so that would be a nice change of pace. Much better than organizing volunteer opportunities and "community activities." Whatever the school could pay for—as long as it was approved by the deans—we could do. But it was hard getting everyone to agree on one thing.

I was rounding the corner when someone called my name. I turned around annoyed; I was already late. Brian was coming down the hall in a wife beater and basketball shorts. I smiled and leaned against the wall beside me.

"You going to a formal dinner?"

"Hah, no. I'm gonna shoot around for a bit before I go home." He came up to me and hugged me.

"Kay. So what's up?"

He spoke with his arms still around me. "Prom. Heard you guys are starting to plan it?" I nodded. "Got any good ideas?" He squeezed me tighter.

"No good ideas. I'm late though, I'll see you later." I weaved my way out of his embrace.

He smiled. "Okay," he said. I blew him a kiss and continued walking to the classroom in the Social Studies hall where we were meeting.

When I arrived, everyone was already seated and in the middle of something. The students' desks and chairs were fashioned in a "U" shape, with the teacher's desk at the top, closing the arrangement into a circle. I sat at the desk closest to the door, next to the teacher's desk. Carol leaned in and filled me in. We were organizing prom, which I already knew. They had split into partners to work on specific tasks. They were currently discussing prom theme ideas. The teacher in charge of the meeting, who was now listening to the different ideas and nodding contemplatively as the students discussed and argued, had all of the pairs written down in front of her.

"We're all paired already. Peyton's with Stephanie."

"Great, so I'm working with you?" I asked Carol, trying to peek over at the sheet the teacher had. She didn't answer right away, but only looked across the room, then looked down awkwardly. I turned my head in the direction her eyes had pointed, to the girl she was looking at. The girl with the skin torn and repaired in so many places. Caramel skin like the perfect tan, but put through too much torment to ever be considered beautiful to society. She was sitting across the room looking down at a pencil. She was rolling it back and forth across the table, leaned back like she was waiting for a bus. No way.

"No. Be serious, who am I working with?" Carol just looked at me, trying to gage my anger. "Well, who are *you* working with?"

She struggled for words. "Um, I'm working with Jason." She looked over to the lanky kid, and he winked at her. She turned back around to me with a goofy smile, then she saw my face and it fell. "Well, you were late, and everyone already picked so you . . . . Sorry." She saw that she wasn't helping and quickly went back so she was sitting upright in her chair. I couldn't believe it. Carol was supposed to be one of my best friends. In fact, most of my friends were here. They knew I was coming and no one thought to wait for me? Or volunteer to be my partner?

After she finished her thought, the teacher in charge of the event welcomed me to the meeting, "We are planning prom and have already split into partners. Your partner is—"

"I know," I cut her off. Then I looked over to the girl pushing her pencil back and forth. "I'll work with you, but I get to decide what we do."

Everyone looked at her. It took a solid 5 seconds for her to respond to my demand. She breathed in and out, and then glanced up. For a second, she looked startled that people were looking at her. I could tell she had no idea what I just said. I was so annoyed with her.

"I'll work with you. But I'm deciding what we do," I repeated.

She lifted her eyebrows and looked at me a minute. Then her face went back to the dull expression she always wore and she shrugged as if saying, "Go right ahead." Then she looked back down and went back to her mission to roll the crap out of that pencil. Then everyone turned to me.

"So, what are we doing about this theme?" Then the conversation started right back up again. I shook my head. Why are they all so easily distracted?

So many ideas flew around, and they all sucked. Nonsense about vampires, mermaids, decades, leprechauns, even fruit. A lot of the suggestions were cliché and cheesy, or just weird. I was still steaming over being shafted to work with the odd ball. This is why I noticed her stop with the pencil and suddenly shift her focus to the window. She just looked up at the sky for a minute, and then returned her eyes to the table, furrowing her eyebrows as if contemplating something important. Suddenly the girl with the pencil said something.

"What about stars. Like the ones in the sky." She was still talking to the pencil. Everyone turned towards her, stunned like they had just witnessed the coming of a messiah. No one in the room had ever heard her speak, except for the few who had known her a little longer than the four years of high school. She elaborated no further, and once everyone finally got over the shock of hearing that girl speak, they started to consider her idea. It was brilliant. 'Stars' wasn't exactly a theme, but there were so many different things you could do with that. I could just picture a gym that would otherwise be shrouded in darkness lit only by the tiny yet powerful little bulbs resembling the familiar stars that fill the night sky. There was the element of mystery and romance that went hand in hand with a starry night, along with the fun and adventurous possibilities that could be introduced. We could bring light to the constellations, astronomy, or even those gods that were thought to live among the stars. It was creative and had never been done before. It was perfect for our school— for our senior prom.

But of course, no one else could see that. They obviously really didn't understand the brilliance of it. They nodded their heads in consideration but no one took her suggestion seriously. They acknowledged the fact that she spoke and treated it like an animal at the zoo. She was a great exhibition, but it was time to move on to the next exhibit. In their thoughts, they had all already begun to move on, but no one wanted to break the silence that had taken over the room. These students are lucky to have me to help them make important decisions.

"I love it," I said simply. "Stars." All eyes on me again. "There's a lot we could do with that: starry night, the constellations, the romance that comes along with it. It's perfect." They all agreed with me, of course. The teacher smiled and nodded her head. She asked if that theme was fine with everyone, it was. She wrote it down. And then it was settled. 'Stars' was the theme for our senior prom. She then suggested that we go ahead and get started on the planning and decorations. She wrote tasks on the board. As she was writing, I took a lighter out of my pocket and flicked it on and off under the table. It was a habit of mine. I was thinking about this dance and working with the weird girl. It sucked that I had to work with her, that I had been abandoned by my friends. She had always been odd. But she used to be less so . . . she just didn't know how to talk to people, to make them listen, like I did. In fact, she was very pretty in the face, gorgeous even, with her wide-set eyes and slender nose. There used to be only *one* thing that set her apart, and would have set me apart if I weren't so sociable. Now there's a myriad of things.

I remembered a day in the seventh grade. I felt bad for her that day. It was so awful to remember. Kids will believe anything you tell them.

Carol nudged me and woke me up out of my reverie. She told me to stop with the lighter, "One day you're going to burn down the whole school." I flipped the lighter off and put it back in my pocket. Everything was listed on the board. Some were already crossed out. I looked among the items that were not crossed out—tasks that were not yet chosen—for anything remotely interesting. I saw what I wanted was not crossed off yet. We were telling the teacher what task we wanted in order, going around the room starting at the other end, so I would have been last. I raised my hand quickly before mine got taken.

"We're doing lighting," I said. The teacher hesitated, then asked if everyone was okay with that. No one challenged me. She wrote it down on the pad next to me and my partner's name. I looked over to my partner. She didn't even so much as look up. She just played with her pencil for the remainder of the short meeting.

Richard's Burden

After the meeting was over, I caught up to my partner in the parking lot. I felt I needed to include her in my planning, not that I thought she would be any help. It was honestly because I felt bad for her, and something else. I met her by her car. I told her she could come over to my house one day over the weekend and search for theme lighting and cool effects to affect the mood of the prom goers. Each group was given a budget, so we needed to find cheap deals to get as much as we could.

"So honestly, just come over. It's okay if you want to help out." She nodded without feeling, and got in her car—a silver Volvo sedan. She started her engine and drove away. Although I'd known her for almost seven years, her apathy still made me really uncomfortable. I walked to my own car, clear across the lot. I saw my friends standing in one of the spaces next to my beamer. Peyton waved at me. I thought about pretending not to see, but she was standing between me and my ride. I wiggled my fingers at her.

"How exciting, right? Organizing our senior prom," she said when I got close enough to hear. She leaned on the passenger side door. "It's going to be so fun, right?"

"Right." I started to go around to the driver's side so I could get in my car and go, but Carol reached out and put a hand on my arm.

"Wait, please." I squared up to her. She continued, "Sorry about . . . you know." I shrugged my shoulders and shook my head as if I didn't know what she was talking about.

"Well we wanted to wait for you, but—" I put a hand up.

"Yeah, I got it. It's fine." I got in the car and started the engine, and looked over to where they were standing. I opened the passenger window and leaned across the seat. They all looked at me expectantly.

"Can you get off my car?" I asked. Peyton scrambled up. Then I peeled off.

Like clockwork, I heard about my plight the next day. I went to my usual table and sat down in the pale sea, me being the only anomaly. I sat across from a girl who made a point of rolling her eyes when I sat down. I made a point of greeting everyone else at the table and wishing them a stellar morning.

My boyfriend showed up and plopped down next to me. The girl across from me looked up.

"Brian," she said in greeting.

"Anna," he replied.

He cupped my face in his hand and turned it towards himself so he could kiss me.

"Good morning to you too," I said with a smile.

"Angela," the vexing girl called.

"Yes," I said, baring my teeth. Nothing with her was ever pleasant.

"I heard none of your friends wanted to work with you for the dance?"

"Actually, I was late, that's why. And I'm sure they didn't know if I was coming," I looked pointedly at Carol and Peyton.

"They could have texted and asked."

"Yes," I said with a lilt. "Could have. Though even if they did," I stroked Brian face and looked into his eyes, "I was a little preoccupied at the time." He smiled back at me. I leaned into him and kneaded his leg under the tablecloth.

"Anyway, also heard you found a new partner. You two could be twins."

"Hm, I don't see the resemblance but, if you say so." I kept looking at Brian as I talked, acting too distracted. We kissed lovingly.

"Well," Anna said with inflection. "I'm done eating." She got up with her tray, and before she walked off, leaned down to Stephanie's ear next to her and said in a low voice, "All this miscegenation is killing me." Stephanie let out an amused chuckle.

"Excuse me?" I said loudly.

Anna snickered and went away.

Brian put his hand on mine. "She doesn't mean anything by it, she's just a bitch." I tightened my lips. "I'm sorry about the pairing," he added, running his fingers through my hair. He looked around subtly to make sure we had privacy, and said under his breath, "Are you going to be okay? I'm sure if you feel uncomfortable you can ask the teacher to—"

"It's fine." I snapped. "I'll be fine. It's just to organize the dance."

CHAPTER TWO

The week mercifully ended. I came home and threw my bookbag in a corner. I wouldn't see it again until Monday morning after searching for it in a desperate rush already running late for school. In the kitchen I pulled a box of macaroons from my favorite bakery out of the refrigerator and took it with me to my room. I set the box on my bed and turned on the TV, queuing up new episodes of TV shows I'd missed during the week. I removed all my clothes and pulled on an oversized T-shirt that had never seen the outside world, and sat down on my bed, pulling the box of treats onto my lap. Ready to start the night. Just as I settled down, the doorbell rang. I sighed and slumped, then made a dramatic show for my stuffed animals of arduously getting off the bed. Before I bothered putting on pants or going downstairs, I used the intercom by my bedroom door to ask who it was.

"Your best friends," was the cheerful reply. Hmm. Well, no need for pants. I walked downstairs prepared for a two-minute conversation and nothing else—they were still on punishment for abandoning me. I opened the door to an oversized teddy bear held up at eye level and jumped as that was not what I was expecting to see. The teddy bear moved and Carol appeared to its side, and then Peyton behind her.

"Oh. What?" I said, perplexed.

"We're so sorry!" Carol squealed.

"Yeah, really," Peyton seconded. "We didn't mean to leave you out or make you have to pair with . . . some random person."

"We just weren't thinking. We suck. But we're sorry and we got you a present!" She raised the bear up higher as if I couldn't already see it. They both gave me puppy dog eyes.

"How did you know I was home?" I asked. They looked at each other like I'd said something crazy.

"Angela," Carol said. "Brian has basketball, and all of your friends are right here," she pointed her finger at Peyton and then the bear and then herself. I rolled my eyes and we laughed. I grabbed my teddy bear.

"All right, fine. Forgiven." I tossed my head. "Come in." We relocated to my room. I waddled up the stairs with my new pal.

In my room we played pop music and did some online shopping, finding outfits that we all absolutely had to get to match. I shared with them my macaroons. I had an assortment of flavors and we had fun picking out and trying different ones as I tried to remember which colors were what flavor. Carol always had a bit of a sweet tooth. She loved macaroons and grew increasingly more excited with every bite and every new flavor. "Wannabe" by the Spice Girls played from the playlist on my phone and we sang along, spirits raised.

As Carol bobbed her head to the timeless anthem, I thought about how she was a baby spice double, complete with blonde hair, blue eyes, and childlike mannerisms. The way her eyes lit up for simple things made it seem like it was her first time hearing or seeing them. She made you want to cater to her so you could see her face glow when you made her happy. Somehow it brightened your day to brighten hers.

Peyton was sporty spice. Though the only sport she played was volleyball, she spent the rest of her seasons at the gym and running. She was usually my workout partner. She could always create a workout plan that suited my needs whenever I asked. Aside from being a physically fit goddess, she was driven in anything she decided to do. She had to be on the varsity team her sophomore year, she had to get excellent grades, she had to dominate in any extracurriculars she was a part of. She wouldn't stand for less from others or from herself. And if it was something new to her, she wouldn't sleep until she mastered it. I remember when we started playing junior varsity volleyball together freshman year. It was her first time ever playing competitively, and she was awful. Couldn't aim the ball to save her life. Could barely get the ball over the net, let alone in bounds. The first week I was so grateful for her; at least I would never be the worst one on the team, so I thought. But she came to practice an hour early every day just to volley with herself, and serve ball after ball until she learned the right technique and amount of power it took to hit the ball not only over the net, but to exactly where she needed it to go. By the time we had our first game of the season, she was a starter, and only taken out of the game when she was visibly exhausted. Same when she made it on the varsity team. I applauded her drive though I could never match it.

"Such a good song!" Carol said adoringly when it ended. "What other Spice Girls songs do you have?"

"Are you in a *Spice* mood?"

"Always." As she wished, I proceeded to play the entire *Spice* album. Grudge forgotten, we listened to the music and looked at clothes and talked about boys well into the night.

CHAPTER THREE

Half my face was smashed against my pillow. I was supposed to sleep in today, just like any other Saturday, but mom was calling my name up the stairs. Why? I dragged myself out of my bed and went to the door to ask what was wrong.

"Company," she shouted back up.

Great. So I actually had to wake up. I assumed Brian, since I hadn't made any plans with friends. I went to the bathroom to brush my teeth and splash my face, threw on some clothes, and went downstairs, running my fingers through my hair as a brush. Before I reached the landing, I could see her standing there. I hesitated mid-step when I saw her. The blood drained from my face I was so shocked to see her. If my hand hadn't been clutching the banister so hard, I would have run back up the stairs. I brought myself back and gave her a skeptical look.

"Look who's here!" my mom was squealing. "I feel like I haven't seen you in years! How have you been? Are you hungry?" The girl tried to say she was fine, but her politeness was no match for Mom's pushiness. "I'm going to get you some lasagna, you like that?"

She smiled and nodded, and mom was off to the kitchen. Mom knew her from middle school, back when she was remotely liked. We played soccer together, and our moms were both the carpool and after-game snack queens.

"Can I help you?" I said.

"Not really," she said slowly. "But I can help you . . ." I was still looking at her funny. "With the prom decorations? You asked me to come over."

"Yeah," I remembered. "I know why you're here. I just wasn't expecting you to actually come."

She shrugged. "Well, do you want me to leave?"

I shook my head, "No . . . um, come upstairs . . . to my room." I led the way.

In my room I invited her to sit on my bed. I was still getting over the shock of actually having her here. It had been years since I had an actual conversation with her before Wednesday after the meeting, and even that was one-way. I showed her some pictures online, and some drawings of what I thought the lighting should look like. I already had a complete vision in my head, and I would do my best to get there. She nodded through all of them, and hardly had anything to say. I quickly became aggravated, and tried my best to dig a full sentence out of her. It wasn't that I needed her opinion, but it would be nice if she could pretend that she was at all interested. This was a big deal to me, and she was being so rude. She was so apathetic about everything.

I threw the magazine where there was a picture I was trying to show her down on the bed. "Do you care at all about this prom? Or anything that we do at school?"

She was taken aback, but it seemed like she actually thought about the question. She shook her head earnestly. I asked why, then, was she even on the committee?

"My parents wanted me to do something, get involved in the school. They signed me up."

I thought about that. It made sense; her parents were always so peppy despite their dull daughter. I could imagine her mom begging her to get out of the house and do something.

"Well since you're on the committee now, put some effort into it. The point is for you to be *helpful*, not for you to be useless somewhere other than at home." She looked at me for a moment with seemingly no change in facial expression, then she laughed and shook her head. I was about to ask her what was funny, but then she sifted through the pictures on the bed, found one of my drawings, and pointed at it.

"Turning the ceiling of the gym into a starry sky is nice, but it would be tedious and stupid to hang up a bunch of tiny light bulbs one by one. You should attach the bulbs to a net, and like space them out, then hang the net up on the ceiling."

I looked at my drawing with the bulbs hung up by string to the ceiling, and realized how stupid that would have been. I looked back up at her, and she had a little smile on her face. Despite the annoyance I felt with her self-importance, I saw that she actually listened to what I said, and was trying to help.

"I would have thought of that eventually," I started, "but thanks, that wasn't completely useless."

CHAPTER FOUR

"You're jittery," Richard started the conversation, as I put my books back in my bag after class.

"What? Am I?" I hadn't taken note of my body, or the vibes it was giving off.

"You stayed awake that *entire class*," he exaggerated his words.

"Oh," I chucked. We made our way out of the classroom and into the hallway. "I guess I did." I guess I seemed contemplative.

He peered at me. "You all right?" I looked back at him and bit my lip.

I don't know what it was about Richard, but I always felt like I could be more open with him than with anybody else. He wasn't necessarily handsome; he was attractive, but he had a baby face. His eyes were green with hazel, not piercing like Brian's. He was kind, and looked so. If he was a stranger on the street you would automatically like him; very approachable, not at all intimidating. And once he spoke his words were enticing, intelligent. Made you want to listen. He made you want to respond even if you were normally introverted.

I slowed enough to hold a conversation, hand trailing the strap on my bag. "I was late to the last activity committee meeting, and you know we're planning prom?" That part had a little excitement. He nodded. "Well anyway I was late and we had partnered up to do designated tasks. Only by the time I got there all of my friends were partnered up with each other or other people and I didn't get to pair up with any of them. I had to work with someone else."

"Wow you poor thing," he said with no inflection.

"No, ugh," I sighed with frustration. I looked away. "Not the point. So I got paired with this . . . girl . . . and it's just going to be so awkward. You don't understand."

"Well," Richard said in his dad voice. "Maybe this is a chance for you to get to know someone new. You know, expand your horizons, network. You've never been afraid to meet new people before; approach her how you would anyone else. I can't see you being nervous about being social. But," he scrunched his eyes and wiggled his head from left to right in confusion. "Who are we talking about?"

"Kaitlyn . . ."

He paused, then his eyebrows raised, surprised at hearing the name. "May? Wow."

I could never tell if he just pretended not to know the gossip, or really was that coolly detached. Either way, maybe that's why he was so much easier to talk to; we could just have an honest unbiased conversation.

"Yes, Kaitlyn May. And she's so *weird*." He gave me a monotone face. "Well . . . to be *nice*, I asked if she wanted to come over last week, to help brainstorm decorations," I turned and looked at him pointedly, "and she *did*."

Richard matched my drama, "Did she murder you?" My shoulders fell at his mocking me. "Look," he continued. "Just because she has a reputation that doesn't fit in your perfect popular princess world, doesn't mean she's not a person."

"Richard." He gave me a mockingly inquisitive look. "I just don't think that it's a good idea for us to be working together. Not *only* because she's a loser, but because . . ." Well, now I couldn't tell him what I was really thinking. "Because I really care about putting my time and energy into this dance and I don't think she's truly into it. She even said she's only in the committee because her parents made her join."

His mocking turned to sincerity. He thought. "Well, again, I think you should just talk to her and get to know her. She's probably just using that as an excuse, because at the end of the day, she could have said 'no'. To her parents *and* you. But she didn't. So maybe she is just looking for a way in, and a good opportunity to do so. You could be that opportunity." I thought about that. "I wouldn't shut her down just yet. Give her a chance. Hey, but, it's Wednesday, aren't you going to be late for the meeting again?"

I looked at my watch. "Yes, but it doesn't really matter now, does it?" I said goodbye and scampered off, with opportunities and excuses in my mind.

At this meeting, each pair discussed what they intended to do about their task. We were given the okay to buy what we needed. This time after the meeting, she met me at my car. Carol and Peyton were with me, of course—Peyton on her way to her own car and Carol with me to mine; I offered to drive her back to the dorm since it was on the other side of campus and she walked over.

When Carol saw her as we were walking up, she whispered, "Are you taking *her* home too?"

I laughed, "No. I don't know what she wants." She furrowed her eyebrows.

As we approached the car, I saw that the girl was back to wearing the lethargic look on her face. Good, I matched it.

"Hi. What's up?" I asked her.

"This Saturday do you want to come over to *my* house this time? We can see what we need to buy, then go to the stores and see what we can find." A panic swept through me and I ignored it.

Peyton said to me quietly, "This time . . .?"

I told them, "She came to my house last Saturday to help me with the lighting ideas," then I responded to my partner, "Sure. I'll be there around 1:00."

She nodded back, and headed to her own car.

"Weird," Peyton said. "Well, I'll see you guys tomorrow."

"Yeah, bye," Carol and I waved, then got in my car. The ride was only a couple minutes but she was pretty quiet, which I appreciated. Usually she never shut up. So I went ahead and turned the music up.

The next day at lunch, I sat with Carol, Peyton, Brian, Richard, Anna, and Stephanie, as I usually did. I walked in with Carol as she filled me in about how a boy in her English class asked her to the dance. It sounded very familiar; I'd heard it twenty times before from different people at different times. I sat at the empty seat next to Peyton where Brian sat on the other side. He started playing footsie with me under the table. We smiled at each other. Carol pulled the chair out and sat down in the empty seat to the left of me. I noticed as we sat down that the table got quieter. Of course, Carol didn't; she kept going on and on about that boy before Anna cut her off to talk to me.

"So, I heard you and your committee partner are really hitting it off," she said.

I paused. "What?"

She leaned in. "You guys hung out at your house?"

"I heard you guys had a lot of fun," Stephanie chimed in, and Anna laughed along with her. I looked at Peyton, who just looked down at her food awkwardly. Of course, Peyton . . . .

"We were just talking about how odd she was, but apparently you two make a great pair." Only Anna would be brave enough to try and push my buttons.

I sighed. "It was really odd actually," I said, not showing that I was moved. "She just showed up, wanting to help. I mean, of course, I appreciated it. But it was really surprising; I didn't even know she knew where I lived."

Out of the corner of my eye, I saw Richard's head pop up as I spoke and I felt his eyes on me. I prayed he wouldn't say anything, but of course: "Didn't you ask her to come over?" he said, knowing the answer. I looked at him resentfully. Just because I told him everything didn't mean I needed everyone else to know. He continued, "So not only are you going to ignore what I said, but you're going to pretend like her coming over was completely random?"

I glanced at Brian, who was looking at Richard questioningly. "What are you talking about?" I glared at him, and he shook his head at me.

"You're such a dumbass, Ang." He got up with his tray. We all watched him dump it and leave the dining hall, bag slung over one shoulder.

"*Anyway*," I said, turning back to the table, "she turned out to be pretty helpful. She had some solid ideas." I looked at Anna as I spoke, my face remaining stoic. Anna just looked back at me with eyes a little squinted. I have no idea what her vendetta was against me, but I welcomed the challenge. Before anything else could be said on the subject however, I added, "How far did any of you get in your planning?" addressing the table. Then I had to listen to a montage of stupid ideas and silly opinions and pretend to be interested. All the while, Anna was still giving me looks. And all the while, I ignored them. I turned to Carol, who was looking at a J. Crew catalog. I looked on with her, until I spotted a beige top.

I pointed my finger at the page and said, "Get that."

She winced and said, "That's so expensive."

"So? It's gorgeous. And it matches the Juicy bracelet I got you. Plus, you won't look too bad in it."

She bit her lip.

"Sometimes you have to give yourself a gift." I took the catalogue from her hands and folded the pages back to make a permanent crease, then inspected it further for a moment. I handed it back to her.

"Buy it."

"Okay," she responded. Peyton leaned over to me.

"Hey, I'm sorry I told—"

"Don't worry about it," I ordered, and continued to listen to the droning teens.

I was so thankful when lunch was over and it was time to go to class.

CHAPTER FIVE

That Saturday, I woke up feeling so conflicted. I was debating whether or not to accept the invitation to go to my partner's house. I did not want another repeat of the lunch debacle, and if I hung out with her too much, then I would definitely run in to some trouble. I had worked hard to gain status at my school, and I wasn't about to let a petty thing like this get in the way of that. But this dance was also incredibly important to me, and as much as I hated admitting it, I needed her help with the planning *and* the shopping. If I was going to get everything I wanted to, I needed her deep pockets. I put my pillow over my face and breathed into it. I looked at my wrist-watch. 11:30. I sighed and rolled out of bed. Even if I did get crap for this later, at least the dance would be the highlight of the senior class' high school experience, thanks to me.

I made it to her house right at 12:58. I stepped out of the car and took in the house. It was the same one she'd lived in since middle school, but I didn't remember it being as big. It was a Mediterranean style house sitting on a 5-acre lot, with columns on the porch supporting the second-floor balcony, which held an outdoor table with four white chairs around it. And on the porch on the first floor was that swinging chair, slowly moving back and forth as it complied with the quiet and gentle wind. I walked up the multi-colored cobblestone steps, and rang the doorbell. I peered through the windows. I couldn't see or hear any movement in the house and wondered if anyone was even home. As I waited, I peeked around the corner at the vast garden that surrounded the sides of the house. Gardenias flooded the yard, all the way up to the walkway, with the edges of the leaves pushing along the cobblestones trying to move them with their tiny might, as the petals leaned into them, trying to whisper secrets to their hard surface. The breeze carried the flowers' smell with it, warm and fresh and generous. I had walked a little ways away from the door, so when she opened it I had my back turned. When I heard it open I swung around to greet her. She had a questioning look on her face.

I gestured to the yard, "I was just . . . admiring your garden. It's really pretty."

She leaned forward and looked around to where I was gesturing. The look that appeared on her face made it seem like it was her first time seeing it. After taking it in for a brief moment, she went back upright and said, "You want to come in?"

"Sure." She welcomed me inside and led me to her room.

By the time we reached it, it felt like we had walked a mile. No wonder it had taken her so long to answer. Her room was spacious and painted blue, exactly the color of a Tiffany's jewelry box. I knew, because she had a couple of them lying out on her desk, the ribbons that secured them still tied. She pulled out the chair at her desk and sat down in it and told me I could sit anywhere. I sat down on the bed across from her. I took the backpack I had brought and put it on the floor in front of me, opening it to pull out a notepad so that we could get started on a list of things to buy. This was supposed to be our shopping day. I opened up my notebook and clicked my pen. I started to write, starting with the netting and tiny bulbs for the ceiling, talking out loud as I wrote.

She stopped me. "When is the dance?" she asked.

"On the sixth." That was in five weeks, the Friday right before we went on break. She nodded.

"*Anyway*," I started to go on, but she stopped me again.

"Well, wait. Are you sure you want to go shopping *today*?"

"What else would we do." It wasn't a question. It was a request for her to be silent so that I could go on.

"Let's go to the pool," she suggested.

I stared at her for a couple of seconds. It was so random, I wasn't sure I'd heard her right.

"What?"

"Let's go to the pool. Instead of shopping or making lists or whatever."

28

"Why would we do that." Again, not really a question.

"Because I'm bored and the dance isn't for another month. We have plenty of time to go shopping. We should do something more fun."

"You asked *me* to come over. For this." I motioned at my list.

"I know, but I didn't expect it to be so boring, and it's such a nice day outside," she looked out her window longingly, then back at me. "Plus, you look like you could use some sun; you're a little whitewashed." I kept on staring at her. I was baffled.

"It is freezing outside," I said with emphasis. *Lunatic. I knew this was a bad idea.* She smiled a little and got up and walked to her closet. She disappeared for a few moments in the vast expanse of space dedicated to clothing and shoes and jewelry. She came back out and threw a couple pieces of fabric on the bed next to me.

"Pick one," she said.

I looked at the swimsuits, and then squinted at her. "Seriously?"

She smiled a little broader, "Indulge me."

I kept looking at her, searching for signs that she was insane. She didn't move, just looked back with calm eyes, mouth pulled up a little at the corners, just waiting for me. I felt a little uncomfortable. I wanted to question her again, or leave, but her murderous calmness frightened me into submission. I sighed and looked down at the swimsuits. I picked up a red and gold two-piece.

"This one, I guess." *I will play along.*

She walked forward, grabbed one, and said, "I'll change here, you can change in the bathroom."

I cautiously got up and proceeded to the bathroom as I was told. Door closed, I thought for a moment. *What am I doing? Okay, I will play along with her and then leave at the earliest opportunity. Oh!* I realized I had a way out. I texted Brian and asked him to call me with a fake emergency. I told him I would explain later. Relieved and anxious, I stared at my phone waiting for the reply. When he didn't answer immediately, I frowned; I was sure my host would be waiting on me. I put the phone down. *Christ, Angela.* I put on the swimsuit I'd picked out and found it to fit. I checked my phone again to see if Brian had responded or was responding. Nope. I went back out to the bedroom, where she was indeed standing there waiting.

"Here," she said, handing me a fuzzy bathrobe.

"What is this for?" She gave me a look.

"Like you said, it's freezing outside." I took it gingerly and wrapped it around my body.

"Thanks."

She put her own on and led me out, taking the back door onto the patio. The pool was placed into the smooth concrete of the patio with pearl white steps leading down into it. Little blue tiles surrounded it, and white beach chairs sat in two rows on both sides of the pool. Each chair had a tan towel folded over the back. On the far end of the pool were two diving boards, one much higher than the other. One corner at the head of the pool was separated by a curved wall that came up out of the surface of the water a few inches. The water in that corner was bubbling and foaming.

"Nice Jacuzzi."

She nodded and said thanks. She walked to it and took her robe off. She looked really good in her swimsuit. It was a black one-piece without the sides, so it curved into a line in the middle of the stomach and back. She had brown skin that was darker on her belly and arms because of the sun, and a gash on her knee from when she was six and fell off of her bike and skidded on the gravel. Other than these imperfections, her body should have been held together by smooth skin from her curly hairline to her blue painted toe nails. But there were those scars. They were all over; on her arms, her thighs, her stomach, her waist, all different sizes and colors and depths. You could tell that some were deeper than others. For a second, I felt jealous of her. She was courageous enough to show her past. She got in the bubbling water. I shivered.

"You'll be much warmer in here," she pointed out. I felt very conscious of myself. It took me a second to strip off the robe and join her in the water. But as soon as I did, I felt the immediate pleasure of the hot water and the massaging jets.

"Ah," I let out a sigh of relief as my cold body warmed in the twirling foam. I sank all the way down in it, until only my face was above water. I closed my eyes and tiled my head back, letting my scalp soak as my hair tossed and frolicked in the moving water. I stayed there for a couple moments, allowing my body to adjust to the temperature. Then I remembered where I was. I lifted my head back up and looked at her. She was unbothered, eyes closed as well. Arms stretched out to either side, her head rested back on the wall behind her. She was still but gave the appearance of regality. She looked so cool and content. Here, in this setting, she actually looked like the well-endowed heiress she was.

"Why don't you do things like this at school? Invite people over to enjoy your pool? I'm sure you could make friends if you acted . . ." I hesitated on the last word. "Normal. I mean they would be weird ones, but still."

Her eyes opened and she smiled, but it fell within a few seconds. "What if I don't want any?"

"Friends? Who *doesn't* want friends?" She shrugged, not pressed about it.

"And why would I want to bring any of those brats at school to my house?" My eyebrows lifted at her description of the other students at our school. Her disdainful tone confounded me. I absolutely was not expecting her to imply that she was better than anyone. It made me wonder briefly if she viewed herself far differently than everyone else did. I always knew she was an outcast, never considered that she would gladly cast herself out. Had she deluded herself into thinking that she was more mature and knowledgeable than anyone else and therefore could not be bothered?

Then my phone rang. I fumbled around in the pockets of the robe I was wearing until I found it.

"Hello?"

"Hey!" Brian said sounding panicked. "I'm so sorry I didn't see your text. But, hey! I have an emergency. I need you here right now!" I chuckled. I appreciated his attempt.

"Uhh." I looked up. She was settled back into her relaxing position. "Actually, no worries, I'm fine. But thank you though, I'll talk to you later."

"Oh . . . are you sure?" I looked at her, casually lounging on the other side of the Jacuzzi. No imminent danger there.

"I'm sure." I said goodbye and hung up the phone. I set it on top of my robe, finally comfortable in my surroundings. I leaned against the wall, felt the water pulse against my back, and relaxed along with her.

She offered to make me something to eat before I left, but I refused. I had thought before that I needed to eat less, and then seeing her in a bathing suit made me feel even more insecure. So I walked to the car trying to ignore my growling belly. We decided to meet again during the week sometime to go shop, so we would have something to show for the next meeting.

On the way home I thought about that day in the seventh grade. One hand on the wheel, I flicked my lighter on and off with my free hand. It was my fault, I admit. Even after I had tried to fix it, I only ended up making things worse. I never apologized for that. Eventually, I just brushed it off. I tried to block it out. When I did remember, it made me sick that it actually ended up working to my advantage. Although I knew that, I had never admitted it to myself or anyone else.

◊

Our parents and a bunch of others took turns taking the kids home after each practice. Every day we pulled up to that big house and let her out. Her mom would be waiting for her on the front porch and would wave to the car as it drove away to drop off the rest of the kids. Every day, the kids would stare at that big house, and the dark-skinned mom who waited for her daughter on the luxurious swinging chair. And every day, their envy would speak for them. The kids would wonder how that family could possibly have so much. And kids can be so creative. They came up with ridiculous possibilities. Spies, lottery winners, thieves . . . They couldn't possibly have made so much money off of their own intelligence and merit. And I was the worst story writer. However, the difference was the kids believed me. Because of my comparable skin tone, I guess they thought that I had some sort of obligation to be truthful about my kin. But the truth was, I spoke out of envy, just like the rest of them.

One day, after we had dropped her off, the others looked back at the house, as the two—mother and daughter—disappeared into it. I kept looking forward, unaffected by the wealth on the outside. But my jealousy built up within, and then suddenly I leaned over to the girl sitting next to me. Her name was Jenny I think. I whispered three words that I would regret for the rest of my life. "They're drug dealers." I don't know why I said that. I completely made it up. I certainly didn't think that it would be a big deal. But Jenny looked back at me with wide eyes as I kept looking forward, feeling satisfied that I had torn down the reputation of those elegant people in her eyes. But it ended up being so much more than that.

Like much of what I said, it wasn't a question or an accusation. It was simply a statement. That was the final straw that had started the whispers.

The next day, by the time I had gotten to school, it had already happened. Everyone knew what her parents were, and they looked at and spoke of them with abhorrence. All of the sudden they weren't real people, and their daughter received the brunt of the repulsion. She received the looks and heard the gossip.

No one even questioned me about it. I don't even think they knew that I was the one who started the rumor. Whenever I heard it said out loud, I tried to say that it wasn't true, but they didn't listen to me. They only considered it endearing that I still spoke highly about the family. They were already so sure of it. How could people like that possibly have so much money? And I gave them their answer.

She never even had the chance to deny it. Before then she was so happy, and always so sweet. She didn't talk much, and when she did it was to a small group of kids she considered her friends. That day, and the days following, none of her friends wanted to talk to her or sit near her. She was alone after that. No matter how many times I tried to correct it, no matter how many times she denied it, or tried to tell her friends that her parents were lawyers—fair business-people—it didn't make a difference. They had already believed in her dishonesty. And after a while, she seemed to accept it. But that was weeks later.

That day, she kept on reaching out to her "friends," trying to regain some normalcy. She ignored the rumors all morning, and acted like everything was fine. But she was hurting; I could see it in her eyes. At lunch, she sat alone. I sat with my group of friends, but I was watching her. I saw the boy walk up to where she was sitting, egged on by his friends. I saw him pull green out of his pocket, and lean over to her to whisper something in her ear, as he put the green on her tray. She didn't respond or move. The boy smiled and walked away. And she looked at the green for a minute, and then I guess she couldn't pretend anymore, because she got up and walked out of the cafeteria. She passed my table on her way out and I saw the clear line of pure misery running down her face. The tear that rested on her bottom eyelashes, waiting to join the rest, that reflected the light as she caught my eyes when she passed, tore at my heart. And for the rest of the day, I tried to hide my shame and guilt.

She learned to manage on her own. And even after the rumors had run their course and no one cared anymore, she stayed alone. That was just the way it was.

And her demise worked to my advantage because people looked up to me. Whether or not they knew that I was the one who revealed the secret, they looked to me with respect. There weren't many minorities at my school, and none of the others were as popular as me. And now I was the one whose family hadn't used immoral means to gain their substantial wealth. I didn't have nearly as much as her, but all of mine was clean. So I gained even more popularity and respect, which carried over into my high school, which we also both attended.

Even though the rumors didn't necessarily carry over, her unpopularity did. Like I said, it was just the way it was. Her insignificance warranted it, and then her obscurity secured it.

But that was no excuse for what we did.

◊

I was about five minutes away from home when I pulled over into an enshrouding of trees. I put the car in park. I don't know what I thought I was doing. I just knew I couldn't drive anymore. My thoughts were taking over my head. For the first time in years I thought about what I had done, and I was disgusted with myself.

And I put my head down on the steering wheel and cried.

The next day I spent at Brian's house, worn down from nightmares of myself. He was still sore from his Friday practice. So we stayed in and started a new TV show, both suffering from self-pity. Neither of us were into the show but that was good. Gave us an excuse to have thoughts elsewhere. He petted my hair, twisting the curls around his fingers.

"Brian, do you think I'm a good person?"

"Sure, why?"

"I've just been thinking about it a lot lately." His shoulders dropped.

"See?" he said exasperated.

"What?"

"I knew she was going to get to you. You need to ask to switch partners."

"I just think maybe I should talk to her about it. Work it out with her."

"No, don't." He said sternly. "It's just going to stir things up. Angela, you're fine. You're probably the only person that still thinks about it. Just put it behind you already."

"Okay . . . I guess you're right. She hasn't even brought it up." I prayed she never would. "I'm not very good at letting go of things."

"Yeah, you're not very good at that." He rubbed my thigh. "But you know what you *are* good at?"

"I can guess." He leaned in to put his face close to mine, moved his body into mine. And I did all the things he thought I was good at.

But that didn't sate my anxiety.

WEEK 3

CHAPTER SIX

Tuesday morning, I was in the kitchen switching over my wallets, when my mom came in and ran her fingers through my hair.

"How are you feeling?" she asked. "You've been really quiet since the weekend."

"I feel fine," I said, like a teenager. I took my IDs out of my black Tory Burch and put them in the Kate Spade clutch that was the same color yellow as my belt and the stone beads in my necklace.

"You just seem a little down. You know, you can stay home from school today and we'll have a girls' day. We can go to the spa and eat some Thai food." On any other day that would have been enticing, but I was not in the mood to spend the day with my mom trying to figure out what was wrong with me. I took all of my cash out and folded it once short ways, then put them in an inside pocket.

"No, that's okay. I have a test today in Sociology." I threw my keys in.

"Did Brian do something? You know, I still don't know about him."

"Brian didn't do anything." Lipstick and cell phone.

"Are you sure? You know you can tell me—"

My voice got a little louder. "I said I'm fine." I closed the clutch and picked my backpack up off the chair next to me and left for school.

After school, I had to go shopping for decorations. I had told my partner that we would shop separately before the next meeting. I gave her a list of things to buy, with hand drawn pictures next to some of the items to be sure she got the right thing.

I fluttered around in a couple of stores looking for the things that would make the ballroom absolutely shimmer with romance. I would see beads, bulbs, lights, and lanterns, but nothing that resembled, or even came close, to what I was envisioning. I settled on finding some tapestries to cover the walls. It would look, not just like a starry night, but like we were surrounded by the galaxy.

I went to the fabric store near the mall, and bought troughs of beautiful fabric that fit the occasion. Then I went to the mall to continue my shopping in the department store. I walked around there but came upon the entrance to the rest of the mall, and something caught my eye.

I ended up in a high-end boutique, running my hands along many nice-looking dresses. I already had my dress for prom, but it couldn't hurt to have a back-up in case I had a wardrobe malfunction. Plus, there would be other occasions that would require a dress. And I was having a stressful week; I deserved a present. So, to get my mind off of the unfortunate turn of events I was facing, I decided to buy myself something beautiful.

A few seconds after making this decision, I realized I was being watched. He subtly followed me from aisle to aisle, as I separated dresses and appraised each one that had a decent color. At this point in my life, I had figured out which styles and colors worked best with my figure and skin tone. I was perfectly capable of finding something graceful and adequate on my own without even having to try it on, but his eyes were constantly on me and I figured I might as well put them to use. I assumed he was eager to help me with my purchase anyway. I had been ignoring him, but after a couple of minutes, I turned towards him.

"Will you find me a dress that doesn't make me want to vomit?"

He looked stunned. "Of course, madam. What sort of thing are you looking for?"

I gave him my dress size and the description of a couple of dresses I had already seen in the boutique that fit with my body type, and he went off to find something. I was relieved to be left alone for a moment to continue looking in peace.

The look in his eyes reminded me of an experience I had in the streets of Dubai. You would think that a city that is newly rebuilding itself and adopting Western customs would be a little more gracious to their American guests. Yet, upon roaming the streets of their beautiful Gold Souk, I had the feeling that they didn't welcome me, or expect me to make a substantial purchase. I would go into a shop and ask to see something, and they would tell me the carrot size and say, "Are you sure?" I wouldn't have asked, or even stepped foot inside, if I wasn't sure. My parents wanted to spend some time at the Burj Khalifa, so I decided to do a little gold shopping on my own. They, of course, gave me a budget, but enough for a couple pieces of jewelry for both me and my mom. But I was still told constantly that there were no refunds, as if they expected me to change my mind. And so, although many had told me before my visit that I could bargain my way to the last dollar I had, I still accepted full price for everything I had purchased without batting an eye. Only to prove this point: I will not be underestimated. I think the doubt in that case however, was due to my young appearance; I was a freshman in high school then. But this time, his eyes sent a different message. There was something more to my guardian's thoughts than just that I appeared young.

"Madam?" I woke up out of my reverie. He had come back with several dresses draped over one arm.

I put on my very serious evaluating customer face and went through them, inspecting each one to see if there was any merit to him earning this job. I landed on one that wasn't as stellar as the one I had for prom, but not bad for a plan B option. I looked it over and realized that I actually loved it. It was cut out on the sides, but not enough to be deemed inappropriate for a high school dance. It had a train that could be clipped up, making the tail ripple even more as it caught the wind. It was a classic black color, but the gems made the light jump around and separate, giving it the appearance of having every color, changing depending on where you stood in the room.

I draped it over my own arm and pushed the other dresses back into his.

"You would like this one?" he inquired. I didn't directly answer but thanked him for his menial labor, and proceeded to the checkout. The woman at the counter seemed bewildered to see me, like although I had spent fifteen minutes walking up and down her aisles, she still didn't expect me to make any purchases.

I put the dress on the counter and said, "Just this." She rang it up and I reached in my clutch for my credit card. She told me the price I had to pay. I looked in and unzipped every pocket, but couldn't find my card, or any other for that matter, and after a few seconds of fruitless searching I realized what I had done. I closed my eyes and signed.

"I'm sorry," I said. "I switched wallets this morning to match my outfit for school, and I forgot to switch over my credit cards." She tried poorly to mask impatience. I thought for a moment.

"Can you just leave the dress here? I'll run home and get the money. I'll be back in twenty minutes."

She hesitated. "We need to put it back on the rack so that other *paying* customers have the opportunity to see it."

I couldn't believe her. "I *am* a paying customer. I come here all the time. You know I will buy it, I'll just be right back."

"I've never seen you here before," she said matter-of-factly.

I clenched my jaw. "Can you just put it on layaway then until I come back?"

"We don't have layaway," she said. My frustration became noticeable.

"Then just put it behind the counter for a couple of minutes."

She looked at me and lifted an eyebrow. "Or . . . why don't I just put it back on the rack, and if you find the money, you can come back and get it if it's still here."

I knew what she was implying. "I have the money. I just don't have my credit card with me."

"Right. I have other customers I need to tend to." She started to walk away from the counter with my dress.

In absent-minded anger I slammed my hand on the counter and demanded, "Put the dress behind the counter."

Her eyes widened and she looked around for help from a coworker. My guardian came over, having heard the whole thing.

"You need to leave before I call security," he said. I stared at both of them in disbelief. I was frustrated with myself for forgetting my cards and confused and infuriated with how they were treating me.

"Fine," I said in defeat. I zipped my clutch up and slung it over my shoulder. "The clothes here are ugly anyway."

I glanced around the boutique to see if anyone had witnessed my humiliation. There was one woman who had stopped to stare, her hand still holding up a sheath dress that would not compliment her portly figure. I left with my hand covering my face. I vowed never to step foot in that store again. I would not play patron to an establishment that condoned their employees to harass well-paying customers.

Insulted and ashamed, I went home empty-handed. I didn't even attempt to continue shopping for decorations. I hoped my partner had had better luck.

I spent the entire next day thinking about that interaction in the boutique. My feelings toward it seeped into my behavior towards others and affected every conversation I had that day. The venom in my words was already there, but that day I had the face and the attitude to match. I didn't want anyone else mistaking me for someone that could be taken as a joke.

Before the activities committee meeting, I asked my partner if she got what I asked. She said she didn't make it to the store, and did not provide an excuse. My anger grew.

"Great. So we have nothing," I said, indignant. She looked up at me, in what seemed to be amusement.

"What are you so happy about?" I demanded.

"Are you implying that you *also* didn't get anything done?" She matched my condescending tone.

My blood boiled. Any tolerance I had for her disappeared in an instant. I made my voice lower and I leaned down a little to make sure she could hear me.

"This is why no one likes you, or would even take the time to help you."

Her smile fell. I felt slightly accomplished, but I still had so much anger left in me.

To keep myself from saying anything else and causing a scene, I stormed off and went and sat down next to Carol, as far away from her as I could. Carol immediately started gushing over her partner Jason, which irritated me to no end. As calmly as I could, I said, "Please stop." Her face also fell, but she understood that she was acting desperate, and complied. She crossed her arms and faced straightforward in her seat.

CHAPTER SEVEN

Thursday after school I went to the locker room to change into sweat clothes and put on my tennis shoes. I had to sweat off the anger I was incapacitated by. It started to make my body ache as it felt like it consumed my soul. Harboring ill feelings always hurts physically after a while. Running, doing yoga, and working on my chakra were always an effective means of cleansing for me. I planned a running route near the school that would take me in a circle. Outside, it was a clear day. Only a few clouds broke the blue. I tilted my head back and took a breath in, then started off. The route I chose led me into a trail, where in some parts I could jump from rock to rock. If I wasn't careful, I could break my ankle. But the thought of that only made me run faster and pick higher rocks. The ground crunched each time my feet stomped into it, pebbles grinding against one another and etching deeper into the earth. It was the time of year when the trees were finally beginning to regain their green color, and the leaves fluttered back and forth to show it off.

I ran for two miles and then stopped to do some abs exercises. I slowed down and the crisp air stilled to greet me. I stretched a little, grabbing my ankle with one hand and pulling it up behind me so that the heel was touching my backside. I did the same to the other foot. I lay on the ground and propped myself up on my elbows, in preparation to do a plank. As I raised myself up, I heard quick footsteps behind me crunching towards me.

They stopped in front of me, and I saw them turn around. My curiosity and slight fear broke my performance and I dropped to the ground. I moved to my knees to see a familiar face, and I was so shocked that I froze. For a moment, I saw all of my monsters and demons look me in the eyes. He had brown hair, slicked back with a light coat of gel. His blue eyes looked deeper into me than just the skin on the surface. He held a cigarette between his lips. He took a breath in through it, and let the smoke out simply by opening his lips at the corner of his mouth. He chuckled. He took the cigarette between two fingers to speak to me.

"Still holding on to that fantasy?"

"What?"

"Do you want to take a walk with me?"

I scrambled to my feet in anger. "How dare you?" I demanded. "How dare you even look in my direction? After—"

"Hey," he put a hand up, still grinning. "No need to raise your voice."

I squinted my eyes at him.

"Look, I'm sorry. I just saw you attempting to exercise and wanted to know how you were doing. It was a long time ago, after all. No reason we can't forgive and forget."

"It was two years ago, that's hardly enough time to forgive, let alone forget."

"I understand. I do. But I'm just as tormented as you, maybe even more so." His grin dissolved into mock sincerity. I still didn't move. "Come on, Angela. I come hat in hand." He gestured ahead along the trail.

I rolled my eyes and then looked back at him. He still had a slight smirk on that let me know that my secrets were also his. "Angie," I corrected him. Hearing him say my full name only reminded me that this was all real. I let my anger cool. I walked past him. He smiled, turned around and got in step with me.

"What do you want? You want to discuss it? Do you want me to pat you on the back and tell you that you did nothing wrong?"

"I still love your venom."

We came upon a little wooden bench and sat down. I pulled my lighter out and flicked it on and off. He pulled out a cigarette and lit it up. For maybe a half hour, we discussed school, running trails, upcoming events, anything but the night we met.

"That's a really odd habit for you to have acquired by the way," he said after a while, pointing his thumb at the lighter. He lifted an eyebrow. "I would think you would want to stay away from fire."

I sighed, because I agreed. "It's a little comforting." Thoughts filled my head. "At least now I'm in control."

We were both quiet for a moment. I had a thought forming in my mind. My breath became shallow and my face felt hot, and not because of my workout. I felt the anger I had harbored for the past week or so transform into something else. I realized something was brimming in my eyes. To avoid the risk of being seen in a moment of weakness, I got up abruptly and said, "Well, it's been nice catching up with you, but I want to finish my workout."

"Of course," he said, standing up. "Do you want to run together?" He was in his workout clothes as well and he had come from the direction I had come from.

"No, it's all right," I said. "I need to go the other way, back towards the school."

"Oh, well you know this trail . . ." It was too late. I had waved goodbye and was already on my way. I knew the trail I picked would lead me back towards the school, but I had no interest in continuing the course with him.

CHAPTER EIGHT

After math class on Friday, Richard came up to my desk to ask me for a favor. I gave no reply but pointed my disbelief at him, and let him know that I was not amused.

"No, no! I'm serious," he said. I picked my books up and walked out of the classroom towards my next class. He walked with me. "I've always thought she was beautiful, Ang, and intriguing. Just please ask her if she wants to go to with me."

I sneered at him. "If you've always thought that then why didn't you ask her out before?"

Thoughts crossed his face. "Well, you know." He scratched the back of his head. "It just would have been awkward. I barely know her and . . ." I stopped walking and looked at him hard. His eyes tried to run away from mine.

I read him what was constantly in my mind. "You mean you were worried you would have been judged." *I'm still worried about it.* "You've been telling me all this time how accepting and welcoming I should be to her when you can't even follow your own advice? You were afraid to associate yourself with her because you worried about what others would think, just like the rest of us." I squared up to him. "You act so self-righteous, Richard, like you would never do anything unethical and you act like you don't care what others think about you as long as you're doing the right thing. But you think just like the rest of us, you just don't admit it to yourself. You're no one's guardian; you just pretend to be to keep up your appearance as a saint. Now who's the dumbass?" I started to walk away again. He put a hand on my shoulder.

"Okay, okay. You're right, I'm sorry; I should have asked her out sooner. I've been telling you how you should treat her but I hardly follow my own philosophy. I can shake my head at you all I want, but the truth is, I'm a coward, all right? I still succumb to groupthink and try to stay in line. And even though I can see something's really wrong and I can point it out, I do nothing about it myself, and maybe that's worse." He paused, and finally looked me in the eyes. "I should have asked sooner, but I'm asking now."

"No," I corrected him. "You're asking *me* to ask for you. You're still being a coward."

"True, but you've been hanging out with her."

"I've been working with her," I corrected him again.

"You've been talking to her. I haven't. She would probably feel more comfortable talking to you than a stranger. She might just think I'm messing with her. I'd like to take her to the dance and show her a really good time. I'll show her that not all of your friends suck. Then maybe she'll be more helpful to you." He smiled and nudged me with his elbow in jest.

"Oh, is that what you're trying to do? Are you sure you're not just excited to have another cause?" His charity cases made him.

"Look," he held my arm, stopping me from moving. "I think there's something really cool about her. I just need a chance to get to know her."

I looked into his eyes and tried to read his expression, for hints of insincerity.

"Angie, *please*. You understand; you only started talking to her when you had to work with her for prom. I've never gotten an opportunity like that to get to know her. But we've all gone to school together since middle school, and I've always liked her."

I gave him a doubtful look. *How could you like her?*

"Please," he pleaded again. He put his hands together to beg.

"I don't even think she's going to the dance." I shrugged. "I can't imagine she'd have fun."

"She will—she'll be with me."

"That makes zero sense."

"Angie," he said sternly.

I thought for a bit. A lot of my friends were completely self-absorbed, including me. Richard was the only one of us who concerned himself with morality and ethics. Every now and then he tried to impress upon us his righteousness, and get us to follow a path of goodness and concern for others. Most of the time he failed, which is why we kept him around. Even if we had no intention of changing, we appreciated his ability to never give up on us. He had such hope for our souls it was endearing. He must have seen something in her that impressed him enough to want to find out more about her. But, like he said, he never took the opportunity to follow his own philosophy of giving people that didn't resemble him a chance. A large part of me wondered if he actually could.

"Well, you can't just show up and take her to the dance. You'll have to meet her and spend some time with her first."

He smiled. "I agree," he said.

"We'll do something together. You, me, Brian, and her will go out to eat."

"Yes!" He grabbed my shoulders and brought me in for a hug. I shoved him off. I pulled out my phone and looked through my calendar.

"How about next Friday?"

"Shouldn't we ask her first?"

"She'll be free," I said with conviction.

He furrowed his eyebrows and smiled. "Okay. Next Friday then." And I watched him walk away, happier than ever.

The thought I had during the intermission of my run the previous day was now fully cultivated. I had spent so much time convincing myself that I was better than she was, because of whom I was associated with, and my outgoing and more universal personality. But the thought stirred in my head: What if we're the same? If the roles were reversed, would I have gotten the exact same treatment? What if I wasn't actually in control? I feared the answer to this. I wanted to shake it from my mind but I couldn't.

I was doing her no favor by agreeing to set her up with Richard. It was an experiment for me at the time. I wanted to know that he would fail. I wanted to know that people didn't think of me in the way they thought of her. I wanted to know what I was to them. Most importantly, I wanted to know that I was in control.

When I got home, I looked up her home phone number in my mom's old phone book. I brought the cordless house phone over to the kitchen counter and dialed. It rang three times before her mother answered. I asked to speak to her daughter, and it apparently took three minutes to deliver the message.

"Hello?" a skeptical voice answered.

"Hey, it's Angie. I need you to come to dinner with me next Friday. I have a—"

"What the hell? Is that a joke?"

"What? No, I—"

"Why would I do that, Angela? Do you honestly think I'm stupid enough to go anywhere with you?"

"What are you talking about?"

Then I remembered—the last time we spoke was before the meeting on Wednesday, when I said some choice words to her.

"I want nothing to do with whatever game you're playing," she said.

I sighed. "Look, I . . . hello?" I had heard a click. I looked at the screen of the phone, which read *Call Ended*; she hung up on me. I grunted and put the phone down. I was frustrated but I understood why she hung up. I probably would have done the same thing. I had to get the message to her, in a way that would let her know I was being sincere. I had to talk to her face to face.

I drove to her house and parked in the driveway. I walked up to the door, greeted by the gardenias once again. Their leaves, hidden in the white river, peeked through to wave at me. My knock on the door was answered by her mother. I asked about her daughter, and she replied by pulling her bottom lip to the side and under her top teeth.

"I think she took the trail around back," she said. "If you just go behind the house to the wood line, you'll find the trail that weaves through it. If you just take that I'm sure you'll find her."

She sounded ridiculous. I was going to leave it at that. I was going to get back into my car and go home. *I shouldn't have to go looking for her*, I thought. I was going to call Brian and ask if he wanted to put on a movie and not watch it. But I kind of wanted to see where she was.

I walked around to the back of the house, and found the point where the trees separated, inviting you to become engulfed in their mystery. I couldn't help myself. I walked the little trail for a bit, and saw no trace of her. After two minutes of walking, I was going to stop and turn around. But I moderately wanted to see what she was doing. My pace quickened; if she wasn't around this tree, or the next, I was turning around. I walked for another two minutes, and got to a fork where I had to choose to go right or left. I became even more irritated. I stopped and resolved to turn around and go home. But then I decided to go left just for a couple steps. A couple steps turned into a couple dozen, and I started to get to an eerily familiar place. She couldn't be there. I felt heat fill my mind and shoot down my spine, as my legs were touched by ice that slowed me down. A little further and there it was. My daze and anxiety turned into a feeling of sickness. A shed, untouched by the elements of the world, embedded into the Earth. I stood frozen. My entire body told me to leave. *Don't go over there.* But, the curiosity . . . I walked forward. I touched every tree on the way, my fingers begging me to stop. I entered into the clearing, and the sunlight touched me, painted my exposed skin in questions. I floated towards the wooden structure. I had to touch it. It was real. Flashbacks hit me and my stomach became knots. I choked on them. Then I heard movement. I walked around to the open door, staying outside and putting a hand up on the doorway for support. She sat in a corner, upper body leaning against the wall, legs loosely folded. She just sat, thoughts covering her face.

"Kaitlyn?" She jumped, frightened. I apologized. "I just went to your house. Your mom told me you would be around here. I was just looking for you." She seemed to relax a little but her eyes stayed suspicious.

"What are you doing here?" I asked her. She shrugged.

"What are *you* doing here?"

"I . . . ." I couldn't finish. I looked around. It was eerie. "So, you had it rebuilt."

"Yeah." Her eyes were closed. She opened them. "They rebuilt it. This is still part of our property. My parents wanted to have it made into something better but I asked them to make it like it was." She ran her hand down one of the walls. "It has character. A homey feel to it. Still does. After that night, all I wanted was my safe haven back." I wondered the obvious, and she answered, "I'm not afraid anymore. What could happen already did. And I already know the outcome.

"I've always loved being here. It's far from the road. The only sounds are from the creek, and the trees. I can just sit here, and nothing bothers me." She turned to me. "Usually."

I let my head hang. "I'm going to go," I said awkwardly. It was too unnerving. "I have . . . homework." She nodded, understanding. And I left without completing my mission. On my way home I thought, *Forget it. I'll find someone else for Richard to go with.* I'd get him a prettier, more pathetic charity case.

CHAPTER NINE

I was so glad to be with my friends after that. I spent my Sunday with Carol, Peyton, and Peyton's little sister, Maxine. She was a cherub if I ever saw one. As innocent and unknowing as could be—but eager and ready for knowledge. Eyes always trained on Peyton, even when her head wasn't turned in her direction. She hung on her older sister's every word. *I* never thought Peyton said anything of much value. But the way Maxine looked at her . . . you would have thought she was an Israelite looking to Moses for guidance.

We spent the day in the town center, perusing through the shops. Our town center was one hundred acres, fifty shops and fifty restaurants, one hotel and one cinema. In the very center of this array was a sound stage, which became an ice-skating rink in the winter. I can remember countless falls, and learning how to regain my balance out on that ice as a child.

We browsed all the clothing stores, tested all the makeup products in Sephora, and finally landed on a place to eat that all four of us liked. The time spent there was never really about buying something; you didn't go to the town center with any specific purpose. You went to enjoy the open-air pavilion, the community, the company. We might have seen the movie we wanted to if Maxine wasn't there and Peyton wasn't scared of her parents. Regardless, we had plenty more available to us to satisfy our time.

In one of the locally based clothing stores, as I was combing through bohemian-style maxi dresses, Carol called me over. "Angie!" she called softly from across the store. "Come look at this!"

I turned from my boho selections to the direction her call came from, and when I saw a piece of her blonde head I headed over. She was standing there holding up two black jumpers on hangers. Peyton was standing next to her, hands on hips.

"Torn. What do you think?" Carol asked me. One number was more form fitting, with a deep V neckline. The other looked like a sack. I pointed to the latter.

"That one looks like a sack."

"Okay," Carol said definitively. "That's kind of what I thought."

"Well," Peyton started, "the other one kind of makes you look like a hoe." Carol rolled her eyes, putting the sack back on the rack.

"Then a hoe I shall be." I laughed. Maxine strode up.

"I like the other one," she said, and picked out Peyton's prudent preference in her own size.

"Good then," I said. "Now you're all happy. Carol can be a hoe and Maxine can be," I thought for a moment, "a potato." Peyton gaped at me.

"It's *nice*! It's a nice jumper!"

"Yes, I know! I agree!" I brought the jumper Maxine was holding into my hands to look at it. I looked at Peyton and said, "She will be a lovely potato." Peyton sucked her teeth and we all laughed. But they both got their jumpers and got in the check-out line. I breezed back over to pick a maxi from the ones I was looking at earlier and joined them. Maxine was asking about food. That's when we began tossing around ideas of restaurants. After a couple suggestions were thrown, Carol said, "That new pizza and pasta place opened up across the street from the Thai food place." All our faces lit up.

"Oh, that's right!" I said. And just like that, lunch was determined.

Once we were full, and our conversations exhausted, we were ready to go to a home. We settled on Peyton and Maxine's house. Carol was from Louisiana, so she boarded at school. I lived fifteen minutes away, but they lived just around the corner. In Peyton's room we put on a movie. We agreed on an old comedy. Us older girls had seen it already, maybe a couple times, but it was Maxine's first. The humor was brash and boisterous. The characters were best described as overexaggerated redneck.

After we finished laughing at one family dinner scene where the whole conversation was a spectacle, Maxine asked if that was an exaggeration or if people really acted like that. In my mind I thought, "*Oh, my goodness, of course it's an exaggeration! I can't imagine anyone actually acts like that.*" But I let her sister answer.

"Of course not!" Peyton said. And she could have left it at that. But she didn't. "I mean the only people that would still act like that are . . ." And I knew where she was going with that, and I wished she wouldn't say it. But she did. And it surprised me, especially when they weren't even portrayed on the screen we were looking at. But she did. And then she looked to *me* for affirmation. I don't know if she did so because I was the closest thing she knew in the room that could attest, or if she really felt that I was her confidant in such a matter. But with her looking at me, and them looking at me, her *sister* looking at me, what could I do? I nodded, and said "Yeah," in agreement. Even though I didn't agree. And I smiled and forcibly exhaled air out of my nose and jutted my shoulders forward as if in a chuckle. And I felt ashamed for a second, but then I thought of survival and tossed that feeling out of my head. And they all nodded in agreement. And we continued to watch the movie.

WEEK 4

CHAPTER TEN

Annette had green and blue eyes that looked like the Earth in the sunlight. Her face was heart-shaped, framed by dirty blonde hair. Her cheeks stayed flushed. The rest of her skin looked the color and delicacy of paper. Despite having been everywhere that her father's leash could reach, she always smelled like lavender, as if she was the delicate flower that she looked to be. Annette was beautiful, but she was stupid. She liked to think that she was adventurous. But she simply just risked everything for nothing, constantly. She was wealthy, and she knew it. If she got herself into trouble, she could easily use connections to get out of it.

One of the risks she took was dating Johnny. He was just as "adventurous" as her, but worse—he was smart. He didn't need connections; he knew how to get out of trouble on his own. You couldn't trust him for anything; he was always only looking out for himself.

On a Friday morning, I was talking to Brian by my locker. Our relationship was still fresh at this point. Annette came strolling down the hallway towards us with Johnny's arm around her waist and his hand too low on her back.

"He-ey," she sang. "Guess what we have planned for tonight." She ditched the source of her mother's disappointment to lean on me while giving me a half-hearted hug.

"Hmm," Brian said. "This can't be good." He was smarter then, less naïve.

"You know that shed by the creek near River Drive?" I had to think for a moment, and then I felt foolish; I passed it nearly every day. Of course I did.

"We're gonna smash it," Johnny whispered loudly in Brian's ear.

"And why would we do that," Brian responded, pushing Johnny off of him.

"Glad you asked," he put on his storytelling voice. "The Mays' own it."

"As in . . . Kaitlyn May?" I inquired.

"Precisely. And everyone knows they're scum, with more money than they know what to do with."

"They own it?" I couldn't imagine the lavish Mays owning a dirty wooden shed in the middle of the woods.

"Technically, it's on their property. They funded the creation of the trail by the creek." Johnny explained.

"But why would we mess with their property?"

"Relax, Angela. They won't miss it. We're just going to teach them a lesson about bringing dirty money into our town." I winced. "Plus, it will be fun. We'll make a party of it. Come on," he lightly punched Brian in the shoulder. "We're teenagers; we destroy things and do crazy stuff. No one can blame us."

"'We didn't start the fire,'" Annette wisely added, quoting Billy Joel.

$$\Diamond$$

Those words rang in my ears as I waited for my alarm to go off Tuesday morning. I turned over in my bed to face away from the sunlight. My eyes were still wide open when it went off, but I pulled my covers up over my head and sank deeper into the cotton. My wristwatch landed beside my ear, and I lay awake daydreaming to the tiny sound of it. It ticked away at my early morning, telling me how much time was passing while everything around me stayed still.

My alarm rang a second time. I removed the covers, sitting up to look out the window. The view was engrained in my memory, after looking at it every day since moving into that house when I was three. The familiar sight filled me with nostalgia as I remembered in a flash the many years that had passed, memories of me playing outside with the neighbors' children. I remembered a time when I was little, and the big things didn't matter. I remembered a time when the mistakes I made had little consequences, and fights and grudges lasted merely a day, and no one could remember where their rage stemmed from. Now it seemed to spark from every issue and stayed fresh in everyone's mind, and we all just sit around waiting for an opportunity to voice it.

I sighed, and got up to get ready for school.

When lunchtime came around, I met up with Carol and Peyton in the dining hall, and we went to sit at our usual table after filling our trays with food. Anna and Richard were among the people already seated. As we approached, the conversations stopped. I tried to ignore the sudden silence as we sat down, but Anna was quick to give me an explanation for it.

"Hey," she said with purpose and a grin.

"Hey," I said back with chagrin.

"So I heard you have plans with Kaitlyn May this Friday."

"You can ask Richard about that; he's the one who's dying to meet her." I pointed a look at Richard. He bit his lip and looked down.

"Oh, but I wanted to ask *you*." Here we go again, a chance for Anna to alienate me and push me out of the group. "You two have started hanging out a lot since you became partners for prom planning."

I glanced around to see if anyone was listening. Carol and Peyton had their eyebrows raised but weren't making eye contact with me, just shuffling food around their plates with their forks. Others were looking intently at Anna to see where she was going with this. Richard, the sage, the moderator of justice, remained out of it. In this sea of friends, I felt alone, left to defend myself. I tried to hide my self-consciousness. My hands shifted a little as I subconsciously tried to hide them. I started picking up my food to give them something to do.

"Yeah, so?" I asked, unmoved.

"So will you start doing other things together too? Like rapping? Rioting?"

"Anna . . ." I started. Her implicative questions were making me feel hot. The others at the table tried to hide their drama-craving smiles and petty amusement.

"Or speaking unintelligibly? Hanging from trees?"

I dropped my fork back on my plate, making a loud clanging sound that startled everyone at the table. There. I was moved. She crossed the line, so much so that it caused me to drop my lifeless demeanor. I raised my voice. "What the hell is wrong with you, Anna?"

Words rushed in my head and my mouth scrambled to land on just one. "I can't . . . What are you . . . You racist bitch." I finally spewed out. "Are you so privileged that you think your words don't have consequences?" I stood up and addressed the table. "Have I led any of you to believe that I would sit here and let you talk to me like that? Do any of you think what she is saying is okay?" *What am I trying to say?* In my mind I screamed, *Who am I to you all? Am I some sort of joke? Is this how you talk about me when I'm not around?* The entire table looked at me in stunned silence. I continued my rant, without knowing what I was saying or why I was saying it.

"I'm sick of listening to you all talk about something you have half an idea about. None of you have any respect for others and I'm telling you right now I'm not going to tolerate it anymore. You can't limit your knowledge about someone to what you see on the news and on TV shows." I looked directly at Anna, whose startled face still held a smug smile. "You're fucked, Anna. Everything that you just listed is a gross over exaggeration and generalization; *it doesn't apply to everyone.* And even if it did, you're in no position to judge. And the last was just in bad taste, even for you." I turned to storm away but turned back as more words wanted to jump out. "And you can't possibly think that idiotic behavior is exclusive to one group of people. No group or race has monopoly over what's socially acceptable or not. To push all idiocy to another group just because it's not your own just shows how ignorant and disconnected from reality you are."

Richard finally started to say something, I assume to my aid. I put a finger up in his face. "Don't," I stopped him. Usually this was his soap box. But when it really mattered, when it came down to putting his own reputation on the line, he couldn't be bothered. I swallowed and changed my tone to be calmer and more dignified. All eyes were still on me.

"I've had a stressful day. I think I'll go *out* for lunch instead," I said. "If anyone wants to join, meet me by my car in five minutes."

I swiped my clutch up off the table and walked out of the dining hall. I went straight to the ladies' room and paused at the sink. I put my weight on my hands, placed on either side of the sink bowl, and exhaled. My reputation for level-headedness was ruined, as well as the façade that I didn't care what they said. I looked up at myself in the mirror. I didn't even know why I had said any of that; it just came out of me. Despite my true opinions, I had always made it clear to my friends that I didn't share the same sentiments as others that resembled me, making them feel secure enough to say what they wanted around me, knowing I wouldn't protest. After holding my tongue on political and racial issues long enough on countless occasions, they had marked me as one of them, and not the anarchic others that they see mainly on television. And now I worried that in moments I had tarnished that image. The only way to salvage this was to buy them an unnecessary lunch at a restaurant that served bottomless mimosas and oysters, and hope that enough shining crystal glasses would blind their memory and make my friends forget my outburst—or what had caused it.

After dabbing cold water on my face and retouching my makeup, I went outside to my car. I found the usual suspects standing there waiting for it to be unlocked. They peered anxiously at my face to see if I was still irritated.

"I hope Frank's working today," I said as I approached. "I could use a drink."

They smiled with relief and nodded in agreement. "Anna was way out of line," Carol justified. I unlocked the doors and they eagerly jumped in, ready to stuff their faces and fawn over our favorite waiter who faithfully neglected to check our IDs.

When I finally got home that day, I went straight to my room, bypassing my mother's inquiries, and crawled into my bed, defeated. I had spent the day after lunch gossiping about insignificant people and pressuring people to buy things they didn't need, but still tugging at the corners of my mind was the immense regret of what I had said. In the safe space of my room, I unleashed.

"Aghhh." I growled loudly, followed by a self-loathing whimper.

Oh my God, what have I done, I thought. My friends relied on me to listen and nod in agreement while they said and perpetuated terribly prejudice things. I had spent years gaining their trust and today I had so swiftly ruined it. I knew that what made our relationship work was the validation they felt when I confirmed, even encouraged, their right to feel entitled. They were going to think I was crazy.

Anna had hated me ever since Brian and I got into a relationship; she never thought I was good enough for the group. I counteracted this by making everyone feel empowered and pulling favors for them using my parents' money, and proving that I was everything opposite of what they said of people that looked like me. She constantly challenged me, pointed out every mistake I made. I always trod so carefully when she was around. I put up a veil of confidence and indifference, as if her insults weren't offensive to me. I dropped my veil that day. But what did I reveal?

I thought and thought of a way to fix this. I figured the only way this wouldn't seem like a random temper tantrum would be if I continued to prove my point, though in a less dramatic way. Maybe I could introduce Kaitlyn into the group as a gateway? Then once they got to know her, they would see what I see—a regular human being. Then they would know I wasn't crazy and we all could be friends. As I lay there coming up with a game plan, I came to the realization that no matter how I spun it, in order to stand by my own incriminating words, I had to hang out with her. It wouldn't make sense for me to defend our association and then continue to treat her like a leper. I had to let her in. I wouldn't be hanging out with anyone that didn't fit into their criteria. I had to secure my reputation and show them that she was more like me. The double-date dinner with Richard would be a good start.

I turned the idea around in my mind. I wondered if I was strong enough to hold her in my presence for an extended period of time. For the past couple of years, every time I acknowledged her I went into a self-loathing depression. She triggered something in me that made me regret ever looking at her. I feel ashamed that I used her as a stepping stone to get to where I was, but I felt angry that she was so pathetic and allowed herself to be utilized. My blood boiled just thinking about it. Why doesn't she fight back? How am I supposed to feel sorry for someone who can't even help herself? She is always in the worst way: helpless. Giving up. We've dragged her and her reputation through the mud for years, but why can't she just get up out of the dirt and stand up for herself? She's so pathetic, she completely deserved—

Knock, knock. I shot up in my bed. "Sweetheart, would you like something to eat?"

My thoughts were interrupted by my mother. Thank God. I was going down a dark path and my heart was pounding.

"Yea, I'll be down in a minute," I replied.

I laid back down and sighed. Why did the thought of her always bother me so much? I've tried so hard just to turn a blind eye and be happy in my status. I am constantly waiting for a serenity that I can't reach.

CHAPTER ELEVEN

Wednesday. Today was the day. I had the activities committee meeting after school. I had to convince her to go to dinner with Richard, and convince Brian to go to make it a double date. A sick feeling washed over me as I thought about the day I had ahead of me. But I thought about the scene I made at lunch. I had to make this work. I felt like my mouth had made a decision that my mind had not yet agreed to.

Lunch came around too quickly that day. Usual conversations with the usual people. This looming obstacle that I had managed to avoid for years was suddenly the center of every thought I had. I was nowhere near ready to face my guilt, but I would have to. I had to prove to them that my words meant something. I had to let her in. I had convinced myself that I could do so without letting in all of the baggage that came with it, but I would learn soon that that would be impossible; letting her in meant letting in all of my demons.

School ended. The activities committee was about to begin. I sat down next to her, and spoke without looking at her.

"Look, I'm really sorry about what I said to you last Wednesday. I was just having a really bad day." She scoffed. "Not that that's an excuse. But I'm seriously asking you to have dinner with me and a couple others on Friday." She reeled her head to look at me in disbelief. "My friend Richard wants to meet you," I explained.

"I. Have. No. Interest. In being near you or any of your friends ever again. I tried being nice to you, even after . . ." she flipped her hand, not saying what we both knew. "You're just too . . . horrible." I breathed.

"All right," I said. Though I wasn't done. Carol walked in and was heading to where we usually sat. "Carol," I called. She looked up and when she saw me said, "Oh," and started walking over. Then when she saw who I was sitting next to her eyebrows furrowed a little.

"Are we sitting next to our partners?" she asked cautiously as she sat.

"No, but I figured it would make things easier. Plus, she has really good ideas," I said forcibly eager. Her eyebrows remained the same but she nodded. Then she brightened up as she remembered her own partner.

"Hey, Jason!" He looked over. She grinned and tapped the place next to her with her fingernails. "We're sitting next to our partners!" He grinned back and moved to sit next to her.

As she mooned over him, I turned to my partner and told her, "This is really important to him, he really likes you."

"You think I have good ideas?"

"What? Oh, yeah. I mean that's why I came over to your house the second weekend. But anyway, Richard is a great guy and I promise you he's nothing like the rest of them. We—"

"Angela," she said strained. She looked in my eyes. "If you're hanging out with him, he's probably exactly like the rest of them. Exactly like you. I'm not interested." Her eyes expressed her conviction. I looked back at her, disappointed, but not defeated. I was never good at giving up and I knew one way or the other Friday would work out the way I wanted.

"Right, Angela?" Carol included me in her conversation with Jason. From the way Carol's eyebrows were raised when I turned my head, I assumed I should say, "Yes." Whatever attempt she had just made to impress him must have worked because he mooned right back at her. Peyton had come in and though both me and Carol were engaged in conversation, managed to find a place to sit next to Stephanie.

"All right, guys, let's get started!" The teacher engaged us in her plans for the meeting that day.

After the meeting was over, Kaitlyn picked up her notebook and left. I raised my hand, too late to stop her. "Wai—"

"So," Carol said to me, "Are we going to see the movie this weekend? Finally?"

I picked up my own belongings.

"No, not this weekend, I have too much going on." I gave her a rushed goodbye, waved at Peyton, and went after Kaitlyn, catching up to her in the parking lot.

"Hey!" She kept walking to her car. "Kaitlyn, he wants to take you to the dance," I thought that would entice her. She kept walking. I knew she could hear me; I was closing the gap. "Just come with us to dinner and you'll see he's a really ni—" She spun around.

"Why?" she yelled. "Why would I go out with you and your evil friends?" She caught me off-guard. I looked around to see if there were any witnesses.

"Richard is not evil, he's way different. I know, you think we're a bunch of horrible people and you have every right to hate us. I mean, I would. But he has nothing to do with . . . any of that. He's a good friend, and a good person, and I think you're really going to like him."

"How would you know who I would like?"

"Well, everyone likes him," I said unconvincingly. "Look. I understand that the last thing you want to do is spend a night with the girl who only has mean things to say." One of her eyebrows tried to crawl over the other.

"Or do," she helped me.

". . . But," I continued. "Richard deserves a chance. Maybe it'll help your pride if you remember that it's not for me, it's for him." She hesitated before she answered. "He really likes you," I elongated melodically.

"Since when?"

"According to him, since always." I think I saw her eyes go somewhere behind the sun, and then come back to earth.

"Fine," she said with defeat. "One dinner." I smiled.

"One dinner."

CHAPTER TWELVE

Thursday evening, three weeks before the dance, Brian came to my house to see me. I was looking at earrings out of a catalogue at my desk when my mom called up to me that I had company.

He walked in and my heart hardly fluttered. "Hey." He kissed me on the cheek and sat on the corner of my bed. I turned in my chair to face him. He was reaching a hand in his bag. "I know I'm a little late, but I had to think of the perfect way to ask you."

I smiled. "Ask me what?" Even though I knew.

He pulled out a teal blue gift bag and handed it to me. Excitement rushed over me and I looked up at him inquisitively.

"Open it," he urged.

I pulled out the gold tissue paper and then stuck my hand in to retrieve my gift. It was a glass ball sitting atop a polished wooden base. Inside the ball, two white figurines were posed as if they were dancing, her wearing a red ball gown, him in a tuxedo. The glass was filled with water, and glitter fluttered about and glistened from the turbulence of me taking the gift out of the bag. On the base, an engraved nameplate read *Prom*, followed by the year.

"A snow globe?"

"Do you remember our trip to Rome last spring?" he asked. "Do you remember leaving that party early because you wanted to see the Colosseum at night?"

How could I forget? Cue the harp.

69

◊

Spring break of junior year, our Latin language courses at school afforded both me and Brian the opportunity to go on a trip abroad to Rome, Italy. We stayed with host families, attended classes, and experienced what it was like to be a student in Italy for two weeks. Towards the end of our trip, our host families took us to a ball in the city. After a couple glasses of white wine, I had a burning desire to see the Colosseum at night. We'd gone there for a day trip, but I was convinced it would be significantly different without the sun beaming down on it, and the floodlights highlighting its features at a new angle. In the middle of a dance I said to Brian, "Do you want to go on an adventure with me?" I told him where I wanted to go, and he barely hesitated to say yes, even though we had half an idea how to get there.

It took us an hour to find it, by which time my heels were in my hand. I actually can't remember exactly how we made it, but we did. And I was right; it was beautiful. We rounded the corner of the street the Colosseum was on, and there it was. The floodlights on the ground lit the top of every arch, leaving the bottom of each level still in shadow. The perfectly aesthetic architecture was amazing. I couldn't contain myself; I squealed with excitement. I paused to take a mental picture to keep and take with me back to the states. Brian took my hand and pulled me forward. I laughed and went along with him.

We went and stood right by it, and then, as if we were reading each other's minds, turned towards each other to continue our dance. He put his hands on my waist. I put one hand on his shoulder, and the other lightly on his upper arm. We looked into each other's eyes and swayed back and forth. We didn't need music; a song played loudly in our heads. I moved my left hand from his shoulder so that my knuckles were touching his neck. The warmth sobered me. I ran my hand from under his earlobe down to his collarbone. I uncurled my hand to touch his skin with my fingers. His right hand let go of my waist and rested on the side of my face. My cheek fit perfectly in his palm. Then I felt a couple drops. I gasped. And then the skies opened up. The rain poured down on us. Soaking our clothes, weighing my hair down, making my makeup run.

"Oh no!" I exclaimed. I hid in his chest and he embraced me, as if that would help anything. But it did; I felt so secure. I didn't even really mind the rain when I was so close to him. I felt my breath heat up the space my face was enclosed in. I heard the rain drum against us. It ran down my uncovered arms and down my back. I was supposed to be upset. I should have been cursing that my hair and dress were ruined. But all I could do was laugh. And I felt his body shake with laughter as well, as he continued to rub my back. My forearms were up on his chest, hiding my face. I extended them and wrapped them around him. We held each other like that for a while, until we sobered up completely and finally felt the cold. I sniffled and picked my head up to look at him. He looked back down at me, and moved wet hair out of my face.

"Let's take the metro back," he said. I smiled and nodded.

It was a perfect night, with someone I had told myself to love.

◊

And now more than a year later, he sat in front of me, and I hardly recognized him. I realized that this was the first time that I had really looked at him—looked at what he stood for, in a very long time.

"Are you saying you hope it rains again?"

He chuckled. "No. I'm saying," he leaned in closer to me. "That I will go on any adventure with you, no matter what city we're in, no matter who's around us." My heart warmed. "You're mine, and I love you. Will you go to prom with me?"

"How could I say no after that?" We laughed together. He tilted my chin up with his hand and kissed me for endless moments.

Then he pulled back and said, "But there is a caveat."

"Oh?" I said playfully. "Does it involve an after-party?"

He rested his elbows on his knees and clasped his hands. "You seem to be distracted lately. You've been pulling away, and we haven't been hanging out as much." He pulled strands of hair away from my face, as he did that night in the rain in Rome. "Come back to me."

"I-, I know. I . . ." With him looking at me that way I lost my drive. "I guess I've just been thinking too much," I said. "I'm sorry."

He nodded. "You tend to do that. I'd like my Angela back." Focused, docile Angela.

I laughed lightly. "Won't happen again."

His hand lingered in my hair, and his eyes on my face, squinted in scrutiny.

"All right," he said after a minute. "I'm gonna get going to practice."

"Basketball?"

In response he shot an imaginary basketball through an imaginary hoop, and made a *Whoosh* sound. I chuckled. He smiled and kissed my forehead.

"See you later?" he asked.

"Yeah. Bye."

I watched him leave, then I turned back to my snow globe that I'd placed on my desk. I folded my arms in front of me and rested my chin in their crevice. I lifted my left hand to turn the globe upside down, and then returned it to its resting position. I sat there watching the tiny flakes of glitter float back down to the bottom. They never went in a straight path; instead, each one floated back and forth until it found its way to the end of its journey. The last one to make it made the biggest spectacle of all, catching a current and being whisked back upwards—in the direction it started from, and dancing around for a bit there before letting gravity pull it back down.

◊

Brian Ackerman. He was the reason why I kept A's and B's. Every attempt to make it to the dean's list was because I wanted him to hear my name at the quarterly announcements. He was jaw-dropping. When he wasn't in his school clothes, he wore basketball jerseys that reminded everyone that he was our school's star player. He was recruited to play, and his family moved here from North Carolina just so they could stay close to him. All of the girls fawned after him, and craved every bit of attention they could get from him.

The first time he saw me was at the school health clinic in the beginning of freshman year. I and three others sat in the front room waiting for our names to be called to go and see a nurse. When the nurse called my name and I stood up, I saw his head pick up. When I glanced at him I caught his eyes following me. I smiled awkwardly out of politeness, and he smiled back. From that moment on, by some act of God, he developed an interest in me. He would speak to me in passing, making jokes that weren't witty in attempt to make me laugh, and receiving a polite smile in return, even though all I wanted to do when he spoke was jump his bones.

Second semester freshman year, I did well enough in my math classes to be recommended to become a tutor. I accepted. Brian Ackerman did poorly enough in his math classes to need tutoring. Students could choose their tutor based on their preferences. He requested me. As a new tutor, my schedule was wide open for me to work with him. And also I turned everyone else down. We started out focusing on the material. I tried to keep it just about math, and make it seem like I had no interest in him. I would give indication that I thought he was attractive by giving my approval of the way his shirt looked on him, or acknowledging when he was wearing good-smelling cologne, but nothing more. I complemented him only matter-of-factly, and then dove into the math.

One day he had the brilliant idea of exchanging numbers, in case he needed help with homework one day after school hours. But once we exchanged numbers, all professionalism went out the window. I thought he used too many smiley faces, he thought I replied too slowly. He said he would try to use less emoticons, but that it would be difficult because he was so happy talking with me. I pretended I had to make an effort to answer him more quickly, but said that it would be difficult because I was so busy. I canceled on him an adequate number of times. When we were able to meet up after school I was visibly happy to see him, and finally, after playing everything right, I was his.

I think I only liked him out of habit. I knew what he meant to me from the beginning. It wasn't even that I was in love with being in love; I was in love with power over others. I loved that the others that fawned over him couldn't have him. Having him meant having an upper hand. It meant being viewed by others with more respect and admiration. People valued Brian Ackerman's opinion, so if he liked me, the rest of the school would follow suit. I was already well-liked, but having Brian Ackerman made me much more popular. I became a frequent topic of discussion; I was the star basketball player's girlfriend. And then once I proved myself, with my words and my actions, the basketball player's girlfriend acquired a name.

The day that Annette and Johnny told us our weekend plans, Brain came over to my house to study after school. He asked me what I thought about the idea, and I answered honestly.

I sighed and lay down on my bed. I had been contemplating the idea all day. I put my fingers in the hair atop my head and rested my arm there so that my elbow was sticking in the air.

"I just don't feel comfortable with it. We are asking for trouble, and it's not even for a good reason. We're destroying something just for the sake of destroying something. And," I turned on my side and propped my head up on my elbow. "Who's to say they'll even notice? A dirty old shed in the middle of the woods? I bet those people hardly go out there."

"Exactly," he smiled, and lay down on his side, facing me. "So no one gets hurt. It's more just to have a little fun." He wiggled his eyebrows at me. "I really would like for you to come along, even if it's just to watch. It'll be the first thing we do together as a couple. We need to have a little fun sometimes; it's what makes us interesting." That was the first time he'd acknowledged our relationship status. My heart flipped.

"I guess that's true," I said slowly.

"Please come. For me." He cupped my chin between his thumb and forefinger.

In that moment when I looked into his eyes I could tell that there was a right answer to this, and that this answer determined how the rest of my high school career would go. It was a test of my worthiness to be with him; it was a test of my loyalty to him and his friends. But it also determined who I was as a person. I felt myself slipping away, my resolve getting weaker. I felt my values being traded in for something that was—so I thought—greater.

"Anything for you," I had said. Anything to keep you, and to keep others envious of me. Anything to secure my status at the school. Anything to gain the respect of people with limited resemblance to myself.

My agreement was no doubt indicative of my intense desire to fit in with my new crowd; I knew what a horrible idea it was—the thought sickened me. I had to force myself to go. But then it was done, and Brian and I became closer than ever.

◊

CHAPTER THIRTEEN

Friday after school, I went home to change for dinner. I texted Kaitlyn, Richard, and Brian the name of my favorite Peruvian restaurant and its address, and told them I would meet them there. In my room, I faced the mirror. I looked at the soul it entrapped, and considered its future. I wondered how long it would have to fall to hit the ground.

I went to the bathroom to wash my face. I washed off all of my makeup from the day, stripping myself of my mask. And for a few moments, I looked at my vulnerability. But right before the reality of my life broke through my thoughts, I covered it up with primer. I reached for my eyeliner, and tried to apply a thick cat-eye. But my hand shook so much I had to wipe it off and try again. It took me fifteen minutes longer than usual to finish my evening makeup. I looked at my new face and still wasn't satisfied.

I walked back to my room. My face felt hot as I remembered what I would be facing. I looked at my phone. I had three messages: one thumbs up emoji, one eye roll emoji, and one that was a few sentences long. I rolled my own eyes.

I put my phone and wallet in my purse and walked downstairs. I went into the kitchen to grab my keys off of the counter. My mom was at the stove making dinner for herself and maybe my father.

"Hey, honey!" she said.

"Hey, Mom, I'm going to dinner tonight. I'll be back in a couple hours." After I grabbed the keys I paused.

"If I'm not, come looking for me because I'm surely being held against my will."

She asked who I was going out with. I sighed. Against my better judgement, I listed the people. She cocked her head to the side and smiled in amusement at the last name. I rolled my eyes again. She went to the sink to rinse off her hands.

"If I text 'Help,' you call me and tell me you need me to come home."

She shook her head. "You won't need me to," she cooed. She dried her hands and came over to hug me.

"I love that you guys have been hanging out. You used to be so cute together. You know, the parents at the soccer games used to ask me if she was mine."

"Yeah, because we're all the same color, mom," I scoffed. "I don't know what about that would make you think that it's endearing."

"I know, but she was always so sweet and precious, and you guys got along so well. I *wished* she was mine. I always wanted to take her home with me." Her eyes looked off into the distance.

"Okay, well now you sound like a pedophile."

"You know what I mean! She had such joie de vivre, and she used to be such a joy to be around . . . . I'm glad she's finally starting to make a comeback. You have to take pictures for me tonight!" She was getting too excited.

"See you later, Mom." I walked out.

"Okay, bye! Have *fun*!" she called after me.

Richard was spinning a quarter on the table in front of him. His face was anxiety-ridden, though attempting to hide behind a mask of despondence. I'm sure mine was no different, anticipating the inevitably horrific night to come. Next to him, his full glass of water had tears rolling down the sides of it.

"Where's Brian?" he inquired.

"Oh," I turned my head away from him. "He said he couldn't make it." I believe his exact words were, *"Screw Richard and his charity cases. I'm not hanging out with that freak. Stop letting him get in your head."* Except maybe the word "screw" started with an 'F'.

I felt a hand on my shoulder and I jumped and looked up. It was that freak.

"Hey, Kaitlyn." I was trying to calm myself down and sound relaxed, but that just made my greeting sound like I was on drugs.

Richard held out his hand to Kaitlyn. "Hey, Kaitlyn! I'm Richard."

"I know you," she said, gingerly taking the hand. "I mean, I don't *know* you but I recognize your face."

"Oh, ha-ha." It didn't really look like he found it funny. He gestured to the third chair at the table. "Take a seat," he said. He pulled it out for her, and tried to push it back in after she had already sat down, so she had to lift herself up a little bit for him to push the chair further in, but she didn't hover quite long enough so she had to do it again and again so he could scoot it in more. So they did a little dance of him pushing the chair in and her squatting up and down for what I swear was a full fifteen seconds. I was still standing, just watching them. I almost offered to shoot both of them to end the awkward moment.

After the dance was done, Richard stood fully erect and looked at me.

"You good?" I asked, eyes widened and mouth pulled up in disgust.

Richard cleared his throat and looked down, and then sat down in his own seat. I sat down myself after taking in a breath of calm. They sat there politely smiling and looking at the menus. Richard was the first to break the silence.

He held up a finger and squinted his eyes at Kaitlyn like he was thinking about something.

"You . . ." he started, wagging his finger at Kaitlyn. " . . . were in my freshman English class. With Mrs. Walters?"

"Uh," Kaitlyn furrowed her brows. "Oh yeah," she remembered. "Yeah with the scarf?"

"What?"

"Like she always wore a scarf around her neck, even in the spring?" she clarified, motioning to her own neck.

"Yeah, exactly! And do you remember those feminist rants she would always go on?" Richard tried to chuckle.

"Yeah, I do. She went on a rant almost every day," said Kaitlyn. They were both continually nodding.

"Yeah. That was a good class," Richard reminisced.

"Yeah, it was," Kaitlyn agreed, still nodding.

"Yeah . . ." Richard said.

"Yeah . . ."

And then they stopped talking, but kept moving their heads up and down for a couple more seconds. My eyes, trained on the table in front of me, widened in disbelief at the "conversation" they had just had. Kaitlyn shifted in her seat and looked back at the menu. Her hand was in her hair. Richard opened his mouth to say something and then closed it again. I couldn't even fill the silence for them; they were both so painfully awkward.

I saw red hair and shot up in my seat. I hailed Frank. He grinned when he saw me, finished up with his table, and came over.

"Angela," he greeted. "Hello again!"

"Frank," I smiled. "How are you?"

"*Way* better now," he exaggerated, tossing his head. I laughed flirtatiously, touching his forearm.

"Is there anything I can get you?" He winked.

I took in a breath as I looked over at both of my companions, quickly assessing their character.

"Actually . . ." I deliberated, in a slightly higher voice. "Yes. Can we start with three Long Islands?"

"Of course. Taking it easy today?" he asked.

I laughed again and rested my chin on my hand. "We'll see." I wasn't sure about the drinking capacity of my two guests, but I was not continuing the night sober.

"All right," he said, jollily. "I'll be right back."

He left and I leaned back in my chair, excited about the drinks to come. Kaitlyn looked at me wide-eyed. She leaned in to talk to me in a lowered voice.

"Angela, we can't drink. We're underage!" she said, looking around. "And plus, I drove here!"

"So?" I said with impertinence. "We'll take a cab back."

"And what am I going to do with my car?" she said indignantly.

"Get it in the morning," I said, almost through my teeth.

"She does this all the time," Richard shook his head. "As long as her second boyfriend is working." He sipped his water.

"That's a good idea," I said. I pushed Kaitlyn's glass of water towards her. "Drink up."

Frank came back with our round of drinks and took our orders.

"Extra sauce," Kaitlyn said, to supplement her chicken.

"Lomo saltado," I said.

"Same," Richard collected our menus and handed them to Frank.

"All right," Frank said. "Be back soon." He left again and I tended to my drink.

I wiggled my eyebrows at Kaitlyn as I drank half of my glass in the first swig. She rolled her eyes and sighed, but took my challenge. She cleared her throat and picked up her glass for a toast.

"This is for Angela, who is relentlessly aggravating when it comes to getting what she wants." And then she brought the glass to her lips, and didn't put it back down until it contained only ice and a straw. I cheered.

"Geez," Richard said. "Do you need oxygen?"

I clapped my hands in excitement. "I think we'll go for a round of shots now!"

Forty minutes, one Long Island, and two shots in, I was finally willing to consider myself in good company.

"I've never seen you outside of school. Do you just hang out at home?" Richard asked her.

"Of course not," Kaitlyn said, offended. "No one could just stay home all the time."

"I mean, unless you're just addicted to porn like Richard is," I said in mock disgust. "He'll go home and *stay* in his room, no matter who calls on him."

I was joking, of course. Richard's head spun to look at me wide-eyed and embarrassed. But Kaitlyn didn't miss a beat. She put her hand up in protest.

"Okay, well, porn has a bad rep because the actors are all so terrible, and you can hardly get into the plot," she said.

"That's true," I agreed. "There are only ever four or five baseline scenarios, and when you already know how a movie ends you can't really become invested in it."

"Exactly." Kaitlyn got an idea. "Hey," she said, shaking her finger at me, "what if we made a really good porno, like really moving, excellent cinematography, but still about porn. We could make the *Citizen Kane* of pornography."

"That's actually not a bad idea," Richard chimed in. "But I'm not really addicted to porn," he directed at Kaitlyn. We ignored him trying to save himself.

"And we can invite Meagan to be the main character because she's a whore," I bashed his ex.

"Oh, she would be a great actress; she's probably the most deceitful person I know," he backed me.

"What if she was just practicing her acting on you by pretending to love you?"

"Then it was actually a really great act and I'm really impressed."

"We'll just go to her house and say, 'We really liked your work when you played with Richard's heart, could you come back and star in our porno?'"

We both laughed so hard. Then I looked at Kaitlyn, who was only smiling out of amusement at our laughter. I explained to her, "Morgan is Richard's ex, and probably the worst person that you could ever imagine existing."

"Meagan," he corrected me.

"I really don't care," I said. Kaitlyn understood the social queues and accepted it.

"Well, if she's as great of an actress as you say then we could certainly use her in our film. I think people are just afraid to talk about porn, but if it had real analytical value then people would appreciate it more."

"Exactly! Like in *Gone with the Wind*, analyzing Scarlett as a dynamic character creates half of the incredible movie experience!" Richard rolled his eyes at my obsession.

"*Or*," Richard said, "like that movie that glorifies domestic violence that every middle-aged housewife is obsessed with; it has a compelling story plot but it's still about sex."

I nodded. "Yeah, but our movie would actually show everything; it would still be considered pornography."

"Oh, definitely," Kaitlyn said.

"Oh my gosh, we could create an entire industry of Warner Boner Pornos," I made up the name on the spot. "Richard, quick! Write this down! We have to copyright it before someone steals our idea." I started looking around dramatically and lowered my voice. "And we shouldn't be talking about it so loud."

"Because it's an extremely inappropriate topic of discussion for such a public place?" Kaitlyn pointed out.

"No, because it's a gold mine!"

Kaitlyn slit her eyes and smiled at me. "You are such an actress yourself."

"Man," Richard shook his head, "We'll make so much money," he laughed. "We'll be coming back to the school in five years to talk to kids about our success."

"And they won't even care that it's a questionable line of work because we'll bring wads of money to toss out into the audience," I said, and I imagined cash fluttering in the air towards gracious and praising students.

"Oh, they'll be so jealous of us," Kaitlyn said.

"Yeah!" I backed. "They'll be so jealous of our influence over the industry. We'll completely revolutionize it!"

"But they'll be more envious of the money we bring," Richard disagreed.

"No, they'll be envious of our power! Material things mean nothing unless you have pull." I immediately thought of Kaitlyn and what a loser she was at school, even though she was probably one of the wealthiest students.

"Are you kidding, that's the first thing that people envy. After the things that keep you alive like food or water."

"No way. The most basic thing that people envy is freedom," Kaitlyn brought in a new factor.

"What does freedom have to do with this?" I asked.

"No one would be jealous of freedom in America, everyone is free." Richard said.

"Well, the freedom to choose what you want to be, who you want to hang out with, or where you want to go. If we come back to school showing that we now have the freedom to do whatever the hell we want, in this case because we're so rich and powerful, that's what will make them envy us. That's why people with insecurities hate people with confidence; they exude the freedom they lack because they don't feel restricted. Most people don't envy money or power, they envy the freedom that comes with it."

"What freedom are *you* looking for?" I asked the richest kid in the room.

She paused. "I guess freedom from myself."

I could tell the alcohol was making her more forthcoming. It sounded like the start of a heavy conversation. One that none of us wanted to continue with.

"So," Kaitlyn said to change the subject. "What time is it?"

"I bet it's late," Richard assisted. He yawned to drive his point home.

I opened my phone to look at the time.

"Oh, you're right, my mom has been texting me."

I replied to her, letting her know of my safety. "I'll call the cab," I let them know as I dialed the number. I heard it ring twice and then someone picked up. I ordered a taxi "for three." Then I sent another text.

"They should be here in ten minutes." I took another shot. They followed suit. I asked for the check and gave Frank a hefty tip, just as I always did.

At the end of our wait time, we walked outside and stood in front of the restaurant to look for the carriage. It pulled up right in front of us. I made a grand gesture to introduce the car.

"Your chariot awaits. Goodbye." I waved and started to walk back towards the restaurant.

"Um, where are you going?" They asked, almost in unison.

"Frank is taking me home." I grinned. I pointed a finger gun to the both of them, clicked my tongue and winked. "You kids have fun!"

"Jesus, Ang, you're so shady," said Richard. I laughed as I continued to walk back inside.

"Ang!" I heard Kaitlyn call to me.

I turned around in annoyance because I thought she was about to try to stop me. But she was smiling ear to ear and she wrapped her arms around me. I didn't return the gesture for a moment because I was surprised. I expected myself to push her off, but the warmth that surrounded me was impossible to reject.

She smelled peculiar, but it seemed natural. It was a familiar smell. I had spent a long time trying to avoid it or anything associated with it. It was odd to smell it on her, since I would never associate that or its attached features with affluence. But I suddenly became conscious of the fact that this was a silly notion, because nature does not belong to any certain class. You cannot use a physical feature to determine social standing. It surprised me that I was only just now acknowledging that.

It felt like I was hugging an old friend.

"Thanks," she said in earnest. "I actually had a lot of fun."

"No problem." I said slowly.

Then the moment was over and I turned around and continued on. I went into the restaurant to grab Frank, whose shift had ended five minutes ago. I didn't wait to see, but I imagined my dinner guests doing another dance of Richard opening the car door for Kaitlyn and her being only halfway in before he tried to close it.

CHAPTER FOURTEEN

Saturday morning, I woke up in a funny mood. I had no plans, and didn't want to make any. Frank had invited me to his house party the night before, but I wasn't in a social mood. So, I resolved to spend the day by myself. That didn't work out so well.

After letting myself sleep in past noon, I set about doing my tasks for the day. I plopped onto the living room couch with a box of Cinnamon Toast Crunch cereal in hand and turned the TV on to cartoons. I knew I was home alone; my mother was at a benefit on the other side of the state. And my father of course was God knows where. So, I laughed too loudly at things that were hardly funny and sat like a man in my underwear. I spent a couple hours like that, until I reached the end of my cereal box. I felt around the bottom for anything bigger than a crumb, producing nothing. I turned the box to my face and stared at the emptiness. Disappointed, I put the box down. Well now I was bored and antsy for something to do. I considered Frank's party again. I could go, though I couldn't go alone. I could invite my friends to go with me, though they would require too much attention and I just wanted to relax. I sighed loudly, cross with myself at what I wanted to do. I picked up my phone to text Kaitlyn.

It's Saturday.

I muttered at my own pathetic attempt to act like I didn't really want her around.

I growled at myself again.

I imagined she'd ask where Brian or my other friends were. The truth was, they all needed entertaining, a burden that I didn't have the energy for that day. Kaitlyn was so antisocial that she didn't need entertaining, and I didn't care to make sure she had a good time. I couldn't say that, though.

As I was composing my lie that all my other friends were busy and I didn't want to go alone, she replied.

I smiled in relief. I answered.

Richard's Burden

I thought, *Please don't embarrass me in front of my college friends.*

My mom came home in the afternoon.

"Have you been sitting here all day?" she asked.

"It's Saturday," I answered. "So what?"

"Whatever. Have you heard from your father?"

"No," I said with attitude. "Why do you want to know?" I tested her.

"Whatever," she said again, though I knew it wasn't 'whatever' to her. My father had a habit of leaving for business trips and neglecting his family at home. I was used to it, she still wasn't. He was a smart man. He used to be an electrician. It's hard to imagine him now skulking into people's homes and fixing their appliances. Being beckoned by their inconveniences. After he had a spark of ingenuity, he got his colleagues together and managed a small team of electricians. Then he duplicated himself so that his small team became a company that grew and grew until it covered the majority of the DMV. Soon the money he earned from that company became excessive. And he started buying bigger and better things, and used the rest to invest. Like I said, he was a smart man, so he knew what to invest in. He seemed to have a master plan from the start.

My mother became an add-on once he had developed his company. I was told they met when it was in its early stages. She worked for her father at the time—my grandfather. My grandfather had hired him out to do some electrical work in the office building. My father became a reoccurring character as my grandfather always hired his company because the rates were the best and they did the best work; my father was a great electrician, and great at teaching others the same skills. Eventually they established a contract. At this point, although he didn't do much of the hands on anymore, my father still liked to assess the work that was to be done, so he and my mother were able to meet on numerous occasions until he eventually asked her out. At the time he wasn't impressive at all—owner of a small electrical company in comparison to my grandfather's then billion-dollar industry. My grandfather reportedly let that be well known when they started dating. But my father was determined to show my mom a good time. And anyone could see why she was worth it. She had a full face, always radiant. She looked like she had never been sick or tired a day in her life, despite swapping out a skincare routine for a wine diet. She most certainly could never look old. She loved to laugh, and have fun, even when her thoughts weren't the least bit. She was the type to find amusement in her own misery. They both loved to party, and they did. Then she had me, and I guess he felt morally obligated to ask for her hand in marriage. So he did, and she said "I do." That's where his nobility ended. My mother always liked to throw a good party, but after my father's third liability, the like became a need—a necessary distraction. She wasn't the only one that felt beat out, though. My father had had a son—my older brother—before he met my mom. They were close. When we were little, we all used to play chess. He would teach my brother and I how to beat our opponent in three moves. My brother was good at it, I was not. So he stopped trying to teach me. Now my father shared secrets with him, advice and business tools. My brother learned all he needed from him, I did not. My father and I were never close.

It never seemed like my mother and I were a part of his plan.

"Have you heard from him?" I asked sardonically.

"All right." She was ready to drop the conversation. "I'm going to take a nap." She matched her exaggeration with a yawn. "I have had *such* a long day." She started to go upstairs.

"Mom?" I heard myself say.

"Yes." In her voice there was a slight annoyance at my stopping her. I deliberated for a second, wondering if I should open up. Fearing it.

"Do you think anyone can be forgiven?"

She paused, waiting for me to continue. When I didn't, she prodded, "Context?"

"Just think of an awful scenario. One where the victim is irreparably damaged." I tossed an example out, "Let's say I ran over your baby." My mom gasped and put her hand to her heart.

"Did you run over someone's baby?"

I put my hand to my forehead in frustration. "No, Mom," I moaned. "Just . . . agh." I struggled.

I don't know why it was important for me to address, especially at a moment when she was clearly trying to leave. Maybe I was just desperate for her ears before she went to bed. Maybe I just wanted her to know without having to tell her outright that I was a real person with real problems. Maybe I wanted her to see me for a change. Alas, she took what I gave her to work with and tried to forage for an answer.

"I don't think that *anyone* can be forgiven, it depends on what the situation is. What did you do? And who needs to forgive you?"

"No one, Mom, I didn't do anything." I turned over on the couch. "I mean, do people truly have the capacity to forgive and forget? I know you can say, 'I'm sorry' and 'I forgive you' over and over but are those sentiments real? Can people actually forgive and move on? Is it a feature of the soul?"

"That's a heavy topic for a Saturday morning. What cartoons have you been watching?"

I didn't answer. She continued.

"Like I said, it depends on the situation, and whether or not the person who's supposed to accept the apology can be sympathetic to your perspective. But you have to be compassionate and understand that you've hurt them, and communicate that. You have to be sincerely sorry. But that's really all you can do, everything else, the forgiveness, is up to the other person." She looked at me for a bit, and when I again didn't say anything she turned and walked away.

"Mom?" I heard myself say again. She huffed. "What is compassion?" I asked.

"What do you mean? It's your concern for others' suffering." She knew I didn't need the definition.

"But what is it?" She wasn't grasping my inquisition. "Is it learned or is it innate?" She thought. I continued. "Is it something you're born with? How do you develop compassion?"

She sloshed back and sat on the end of the couch opposite me. "Compassion is learned. I think. Well you have to be able to realize at some point that other people matter just as much as you. Some people never learn that. And there are different levels of compassion. Some people can act like they care about you, but they're just checking the box. They do it as it pertains to their duty or their job, but at the end of the day they can sleep soundly no matter what your condition. They ask because they feel obligated to ask. But for others, they really are concerned with your wellbeing and moved by your suffering. They ask because they want you to be all right. People usually learn true compassion when they realize that others have feelings and they can empathize with those feelings. Others never do, either because they're so self-involved they feel they don't need to or because they don't want to because it's easier." She connected my first question to the latter. "There's no guarantee you'll ever be forgiven for anything. But you take your mistake as a lesson learned and do better next time and going forward. Don't just check the box. Actually care." She was finished with her thoughts. "I love you so much." She petted my hair. "But gosh, I would love it if you weren't so vindictive."

I didn't even give a quip back. I got up and told her I had to get ready for the night.

After spending two hours on myself, I left to pick her up. My mother was still asleep, but I assumed she would get up for a midnight snack later so I left her a note on the fridge:

Ma,
I'll be at my friend Frank's house over on Carson Street. Won't be home until late.
        -Angie

I drove to her house to pick her up, and texted her to come out when I arrived. As I waited, my heart started pounding, wondering if this was a mistake. None of my friends would be at this party but what if they found out anyway that I brought her? Our town was pretty small, and social media made it even smaller. The longer I sat there the more determined I became to cancel on her. What if she was an embarrassment and Frank and all his friends judged me for bringing her? She was so cool and normal enough the times we had hung out, but obviously she was a loser for a reason. Then she came out. Without her conservative and formalized school clothes on and with her makeup done, she looked pretty hot. I was relieved at that. Now for personality. Her behavior was more relaxed than usual. She was walking funny coming to the car, though. She got in, completely giddy. I found out as soon as she closed the door that she was a 'whoo' girl.

"Are you all right?" I asked. She stifled a laugh, calmed herself by breathing, and braced herself on the door handle. She turned to me, face red. Just as I was about to kick her out of the car she said, "I had two shots of vodka before I came out. I was just so nervous! I've actually never been to a house party before." Her eyes got wide as she thought of something. "Is this a pig party?" That completely tickled me. I laughed heartily.

"Well, if it was, I wouldn't tell you, that defeats the purpose."

"That's true," she said contemplative.

"Also, you would have to be ugly for me to bring you to a pig party. And you're gorgeous," I said genuinely. I was surprised I had said it, too. She smiled and looked down.

"That is so funny." I started the car and headed off. "I can't believe you drank and didn't offer me any!"

She touched my arm and gave me mischievous eyes.

"What?"

She reached in her purse and pulled out a pink flask.

"Yes!" I exclaimed.

"You want some?"

I nodded. "Of course. Once we get there I'm definitely seeing what you have." It flashed in my mind that it could be revengeful poison but, determined to have a good time, I pushed that worry way down.

We arrived as the party was in full swing. I looked around cautiously as I parked to see if there was anyone around that I knew or that went to our school. It was an older crowd because they were Frank's friends, but I wanted to be sure. As I shifted to park, I got a little worried again; I never went anywhere without the usual gang. Until she nudged the flask towards me. I smiled and took a couple swigs of it, and put it down coughing.

"Oh my God, that is strong."

"Pure rubbing alcohol." She drank a bit more herself, keeping her face astonishingly composed.

"Let's go in," I said.

"Do you know anyone here?"

"Just Frank, our waiter from last night," I answered.

"Oh, okay." After a beat she said, "You're going to get him fired soon."

"Oh, definitely," I said without hesitation. "For sure. We can't get away with it for much longer. Ready to go in?"

"Yeah, let's go."

Since she looked amazing, she attracted a lot of eyes when we walked in. Frank came up to greet us almost immediately, as if he was watching the door to see when I got there.

"Angela!" He hugged me. He was so drunk already. "And, Kaitlyn?" He tried to remember the name of the girl from last night.

"Yes, thanks for having us," she said, too politely.

"For sure. Hey, here!" He reached around to a table nearby and poured two shots. "Here you go!" He pushed them towards us.

"I will have one, but I think Kaitlyn has already had enough to drink," I directed, as I usually did.

"Well," she said defiantly, looking around. "I know nobody here. So what that hell?" She shrugged her shoulders and took the shot. Frank cheered and joined her in a drink.

After that, I condescendingly waited for her to lose her head. But she never did. She could hold her liquor. And not only could she hold a decent conversation while wasted, she became livelier, more alert. And I learned that she knew how to dance. I fell in love with her. Once I stopped worrying about her embarrassing me, I relaxed.

I had no interest in meeting a boy that night, so there was no one to impress. I had no obligations in the morning, so I was free to shut my mind off, and let the alcohol consume me.

Within thirty minutes, I was in and out of consciousness. At first, it was freedom and fun. My inhibitions melted away and my sense of humor grew tenfold. Then it became a higher state of understanding. The thoughts that I blocked in the daylight started to come out. Of the parts I do remember, I was perpetually unimpressed. Wafting through a swarm of unaware teenagers, just trying to get their next high. I wondered how these people could be so content with their mediocre lives. They gave nothing to society, always consumed in their own drama. Scheming on how to create their newest massacre. They had no consideration for lives outside of their own, and seemed either not to know it or not to care. I remember trying to light a cigarette and being stopped. She told me about the health concerns and the risks involved with each one. And I looked at her. She was pathetic. She was worried about dying but I wondered how bad of a thing that would really be for her. Who is she to society? To the world? Someone, somewhere, loves her. Cares about her. They fantasize about this girl that they halfway know, and halfheartedly try to get to know. I looked at her, and I wondered if she knew what death really was. I wondered if she knew that even the people that cared about her now would soon leave her, either in the death that she so feared or out of disenchantment.

"I think I'll be fine." I rolled my eyes and walked away with my lit cigarette.

I walked through a cloud of darkness to find utter unhappiness and disappointment. When I was at this peak of drunkenness, I was truly myself. Understanding my own emotions. And I realized every time that everything I did, I did out of sheer boredom. I loved no one. I had no one that I wanted to keep around. I saw no one that I was willing to fight for.

I found myself in front of a beautiful stranger. I touched his face. I brought my lips to his, and we moved them together. Only to confirm an emotionless existence. When I pulled away, his expression was one of shock, and the closest thing I can describe as love at first sight. I studied it, and moved on.

At this point I lost another block of consciousness. Frank would send me pictures later of what I missed. A heaviness filled my head while my feet felt light. My vision was clear, but I could tell that clouds blocked my more coherent thoughts.

People became shadows, floating about as I floated in and out of consciousness. I came back to reality in the middle of conversations that I was holding with grace and humor. I heard myself make jokes effortlessly, and become the person people gravitated towards. I came back at one point stunned that I was helping Kaitlyn onto the living room table to dance.

Then, my stomach twisted. My mouth flooded. I hurried to the bathroom just in time to hurl all over the toilet seat. In my drunken state, I remember wiping the seat with paper towels. Frank was suddenly by my side wiping my face. He was laughing, very amused at my disreputable state.

"Why are you here?" I asked indignantly, face in toilet.

"I saw you headed for the bathroom. Looks like I missed the show though." He peeked in the toilet and pulled his head back wincing in disgust. "Why did you drink so much, lightweight?"

"I hate teenagers," I disclosed, not really in response but more as a general statement.

"Aren't you one? You look thirteen."

"They all just roll around in their own mistakes, getting drunk and forgetting who they are. I cannot find a single person that's insightful or riveting enough for me to want to talk to. They're all so oblivious."

"You talk like you're better than everyone else here."

"Well, at least I'm more aware."

He laughed. "You are vomiting into a toilet right now."

I rolled my eyes. "Before this."

"We're all just people, Angela." He tucked loose hairs behind my ear and cupped my sweaty face in the palm of his hand. "No one is perfect, and it's stupid to strive to be. Just be happy and have fun." He looked deep into me. "You have nothing to prove."

I looked at him with pity, because he knew nothing about the world we live in.

"I have everything to prove."

And then I woke up to Kaitlyn slapping my face as I lay in the bathroom tub, because that's where Frank put me after I passed out, in case I vomited again while he went to continue partying.

"Come on, let's go home," Kaitlyn said, as she tried to help me up.

"What if I have to throw up again?"

"I don't care, it's your car." Surprisingly, I loved her for that.

"Are you going to drive?"

"Yeah, I'm pretty sober now."

With Kaitlyn's assistance, I made it to the car. After a nauseating car ride, we made it to her house, where I immediately opened the door and puked on her driveway. I finished before she could come around the car to hold my hair.

"Nice," she said. "Are you okay to drive home or do you want to stay here?"

I stood upright, and felt my stomach finally settle.

"Nope," I said. "I'm good."

"You sure?"

"Yeah, I think that was the last of the poison."

"All right." She tossed over my keys. "Make sure you shower."

We said our goodbyes, another successful night in the books, and I made it home.

I tried to be quiet coming up the stairs, but for some reason I banged against the wall for every step. Pure exhaustion, it must have been. My mom came out of her room, frazzled after having been woken up at three a.m.

"Angela?"

"Yeah, Mom," I answered groggily.

She sighed. "How was the party?" Then the more pressing question: "Did you drive home?"

"Yeah." I paused on the step right below her. "Do you remember that scene in *Wolf of Wall Street* after he took the lemon pill and drove home?"

"Yes," she said, momentarily confused at the reference.

"You might want to check the car in the morning."

She clicked her teeth and gave me an unamused face.

"That's not funny," she said.

I laughed heartily and said goodnight, then shuffled off to bed. I would have to save showering and putting myself back together for the morning. For now, I needed to shut my eyes.

As I drifted, my phone buzzed. I fumbled around for it in the darkness. When my fingers found it, the light stung my eyes. A text from Kaitlyn.

Same thing again
tomorrow?

I laughed out loud, then typed.

I don't see
why not.

I put my phone on the charger, completely satisfied with my night.

CHAPTER FIFTEEN

I met up with my boyfriend Sunday evening at a little tapas restaurant in old town. Parking was sparse so I had to park in a lot down the street. But that was no matter. I arrived alone, a couple minutes behind him, and it was a lovely walk down the couple of blocks. Spring was just starting to peek around the corner, so the walk was breezy but comfortable. I walked along the sidewalk, running my eyes along the buildings, everything built in red brick. The sun was setting on the horizon, red sky to match the red town, everything on fire. The street lights flickered on, illuminating the quaint little spaces—cafés, jewelry stores, novelty shops. Black chalkboard signs stood out front luring you in, telling you what could be found of rarity inside. I approached my destination. I read the wooden sign overhead swaying slightly on an iron rod to make sure I went through the right door. I walked in to find him checking in with the hostess.

"She's parking now." I came up behind him and put my chin on his shoulder.

"Ah," he said. "And here she is." He turned and gave me a peck on the cheek.

"Okay, right this way." The hostess led us to a table for two and put menus in front of us. She listed the specials and gave us a minute to decide what we wanted.

"So, it's nice to finally see you, stranger," Brian said disapprovingly.

"I know! I had such a busy weekend." He looked suspiciously at me but moved on. He asked me how my weekend was and we caught up. I tried to avoid the parts with Kaitlyn—I left the party out entirely, but I couldn't resist telling him about the adult film productions we jokingly planned on creating. Until he interrupted me.

"You've seen *Citizen Kane*? I couldn't see you sitting through that."

I shook my head.

"Kaitlyn said that. I had to look it up when I got home," I laughed. He fell silent at the mention of her name. I sighed. "Brian, we have to talk." I sat up straighter in my chair and braced myself for the conversation I was about to have with him. "I think it would be really good for your mental health if you talked to her and maybe got to know her, or at least apologize to her."

"I've already told you how I feel about that."

"I know, Brian, but I think it would make you feel better to at least get that off of your chest."

"I feel fine right now. I don't need to talk to her. And neither do you." I swallowed.

"I think we should introduce her to our friends."

"What."

"She's funny. I had a great time at dinner with her Friday. Richard did too."

"I don't care, I have no desire to have a conversation with her. And I especially don't want her hanging out with me and my friends. Just drop it."

"I am not going to drop it so, please, I am asking you to get on board."

"Look, Angela, if you're going to keep pushing this, I'm out. I enjoy being with you, and I want to be with you. But I don't need you."

I was taken aback. I didn't expect that to be his response—a complete dismissal of me as a part of his life, just because I was telling him something he didn't want to hear. His flippant tone made it sting more. It made me feel like I was nothing. A disposable object. His eyes stayed steady on me.

Gosh, I wanted so badly to cause a scene, throw whatever was within my grasp at him. I wanted to scream at him, punch him. If we hadn't been in a public restaurant, I might have. A tear escaped my eye and I quickly wiped it.

"Okay," I said slowly, though I was shaking. With anger or hurt, I wasn't sure.

Just then the waitress came with our food and we put on polite faces and thanked her. No, we don't need anything else, thank you. A small joke. Feigned laugher. And when she left, we both sat for a moment in silence. I couldn't tell you what was running through his mind, but I didn't want him to leave me. I didn't even give him a chance to rethink. I was too afraid to. Afraid he would follow through and decide he was done with me. I composed myself. I forgot why I cared to talk to him about that girl anyway. I felt like it was more important to salvage my relationship.

"Okay," I said again, differently. "I'm sorry. I shouldn't be pushing you to do something you're not ready for." He softened a little as well.

"Thank you, Angela. I appreciate that. And, if you feel like you need to talk to her, to find some sort of peace, then I support you." He reached over and picked my hand up in his. I loosened at his touch. He changed the subject.

"So, I'm sure you already know, but Carol is having a 'before-party' in her dorm room Friday. Are you going?"

"Friday? I have to be somewhere after school."

Before I could ask what the party was for, he said, " . . . you'll be at the game, though, won't you?"

"Oh! Oh, of course!" Honestly, it had slipped my mind. It was the last basketball game of the season. The team would play our biggest rivals. And since Brian was a senior, they would be awarding him for being a pivotal member of the team. "It's a quick errand. But I will make it back before the game starts, and to see you get honored, of course." Though I didn't care to. We'd lost the final game nine years in a row. I was sure this year wouldn't be any different.

"All right, good. I'll need you in the stands." He stroked my hand with his thumb.

He paid for the food and we walked out. He had parked in a different lot but walked me back to my car. There we went, happily following the red brick sidewalk. At my car we said our heartfelt goodbyes. He touched my face, and brought his near. We Eskimo kissed first, I smelled him and his cologne. I lightly and playfully bit his nose and he chuckled. He moved his head to kiss my lips deeply. He pulled back after a couple of seconds and said, "See you tomorrow."

"See you." He opened my car door for me and I got in. I started the engine and drove home, with my mind still in the restaurant.

CHAPTER SIXTEEN

In Virginia, the transition from winter to spring has its own smell, as if the air alone was letting every being know that a change was coming. Every year when that smell lingered, I would pause outside with my nose in the air. Then I would become aware that I'd been there before, another year passed, and I would remember childhood dreams and adventures. I would calm my breathing, because if you inhaled too deeply or quickly—if you were looking for it, the aroma would disappear. And the whispers of the past would be interrupted once again, suffocated by the pressures and worries of today. I am no longer a child, but I never noticed when my childish toys were being taken away.

The moment I realized I had grown up, I had suddenly found myself in the midst of a world of importance. Decisions needed to be made, and I found myself ill-equipped to handle them. I was surrounded by resentment and envy and lust, never quite sure which was which.

There is something insidious in all of us, and it goes far deeper than skin color or prejudice. It's the need to be above others. It's the need to compete, succeed, and win. It's the need for compassion being choked out by the fear to show it. It's the need to be comforted by others dashed by shame, and to encourage comradery and in the same breath beat each other down to gain an upper hand.

For a moment I think, *This is all in my head*. But then I hear lies that exist only to benefit one, and I know that honesty falls in second to prestige. I smell fires that never would have started if someone had backed down, and I know that pride and greed are superior to love and relationships. I see people who give up and take indolence as a lifestyle, taught to quit before the game even begins. And people who play in a game that none of the other players know about. I look around at the pigs crawling through muddy water just for a little bit of mercy and I know that it is not all in my head.

I always find myself saying that I want to go home, but I don't even know where that is. I find myself fantasizing about the warmth of a touch from someone that I do not know. I find myself spiraling in my beliefs and waking up choking and gasping for air.

This year, on the day that change wafted through the air, I went to school and came back home in a trance. Because on this day, although I could smell the change around me, I'd never perceived any.

I walked through my front door. I looked around at the home that I grew up in, and heard the cartoon voices of the shows I used to watch in the living room.

I said hello to a mother who used to indulge all of my childish whims with the energy that I couldn't imagine her or me mustering up today.

I ascended the stairs and ran my hand along the banister. I looked at the place on the wall where a picture was painted over, blamed on a childhood friend that I still couldn't face today.

I walked down the hallway to my room. I imagined toys scattered about the floor to the vexation of a father I barely acknowledge.

If I had known then what I do now, I would have asked time to stop. I would have told it that there's no use going forward; we won't catch up with it anyway. I would have relinquished my desire to write the rules of an ethnocracy that I did not realize I was a part of.

I lay myself down on my bed, surrounded by gold colored walls, painted from white to look more regal. I turned on my side and traced the trimming along the wall with my fingers. I closed my eyes, consenting, for the first time that day, to let time pass.

CHAPTER SEVENTEEN

Not heeding my boyfriend's warning, I began spending far more time with the girl whose life I, in many ways, ruined. I was so skeptical at first, ready to defend myself when she decided to retaliate. I felt like I owed her something, but after she showed that she didn't need me to mend anything, her friendship was all that I came for. At school and school functions, I still stayed glued to my group. I still managed to keep my spot on the pedestal. But my "friendship" with them quickly became dissonant as I began to realize how superficial it was. I laughed and played along during the day, but I couldn't wait to go back home and tell her how I really felt or what I really wanted to say.

She was telling me about an idea she had for a project she had to complete. I looked at my phone. Brian had texted me. I couldn't tell him I was prom wargaming with Kaitlyn three nights in a row. I responded,

Sorry, I feel super sick!

"How many different ways can I say 'I'm busy'?"

"Really just one. You say, 'I don't want to hang out with you.'"

"No! That's not true. I just need my Katie Scarlett time." I named her after my favorite fictional woman.

"Nope."

"Still a no to the nickname?"

"My name is Kaitlyn. May."

"It's fine, you'll get used to it."

"You know you've been here every single day this week? He's probably worried about you."

"Oh wow. I have, haven't I? It's only because you have so much good food." I moved to lay on my stomach on the bed, closer to the chili cheese nachos I was shoveling into my mouth. "What do you usually do after school?" I asked curiously. She shrugged.

"Homework. Watch TV. Last week I found out this show me and my brother used to watch is online. It's available to stream, so I started re-watching that."

"You have a brother? I didn't know that."

"You didn't? Yeah, he's six years older than me." He was a little older than my own brother. "He lives in California now. He moved last year."

"So far away. That sucks."

"Yeah, it does."

"What's he doing there?"

"He's a computer engineer. He says the work is really good out there for him."

"Do you guys go visit him?"

"We haven't yet, but he comes home for every holiday. He'll be here in a couple weeks for Easter."

"Okay, that's nice. What's the show?" She brought her laptop over to me and tried to describe it as she pulled it up.

"Anime?" I clarified with aversion.

"Don't knock it until you try it!" She turned the computer towards me and I looked at the cover picture. It did not look like something I would be interested in. But I was curious to see what she and her brother spent their childhood watching.

"Okay, well, let's watch an episode."

"Yeah?" She looked surprised.

"Yeah, I'll try it." She got excited and played the show from the very beginning. It started off with some treasure map? Very colorful and lively. The narration was exuberant. And then the characters paraded onscreen, not regular cartoon characters. It took my eyes and mind a minute to get used to looking at them. Everything happened so fast, it took until I was familiar with the cinematic style and the artwork that I could understand the actions being portrayed. Why are his eyes so big? And what the hell was that voice? My mind spent some time learning what I was viewing. And then excitement happened. I suddenly developed opinions about the characters, who had become subconsciously more and more realistic to me. I wanted to know about the fate of these characters that I had limited knowledge about. It was dramatic, adventurous, and humorous. Jokes that I would ordinarily find funny wrapped in different packaging. As goofy as it was, by the time they said the name of the show in the actual show, I was invested. After the first episode ended, she paused the 'play next episode' feature and looked at me expectantly.

"So? What do you think?"

"Eh," I said, "I'm not sure what I just saw." She dismissively waved her hand.

"It's fine, you'll get used to it." She pressed play and we continued to watch that show all night. We both eventually fell asleep with it on.

In the morning, I only realized I'd fallen asleep at her house because the walls I opened my eyes to were blue and not gold. The show was paused, and the computer screen was asking us if we were still watching. I woke her up. She awakened, startled.

"Oh, shoot," she said, also realizing that it was morning.

"Yeah, we have to go to school." I peeled myself up. She stretched.

"Ugh, I'm tired. Thank God it's Thursday." Thursdays were half days at our school.

"Thank God."

Our extended playdate wasn't really a problem since I'd come directly from school so I had my bookbag with me. I showered in her bathroom and borrowed some of her clothes. I came back out to the bedroom as she was shutting her laptop to pack in her bag.

"We're going to have to go back to the fourth episode, I think," I told her. She looked at me in amazement.

"What?"

"So you liked it!" She'd caught me.

"It grew on me."

"Yay! You know what? I'm gonna show you some movies I think you'll like. You want to come back here after school?"

"Sure." I picked up my bag and we headed downstairs.

In the kitchen, an abundance of food waited, along with both of her parents. I was surprised to see so much food prepared. I usually skipped breakfast or scrounged for leftovers if I was hungry. Her mom was surprised to see me.

"Angela! I didn't know you were spending the night," she said when she looked up. Her father turned from his newspaper.

"I didn't either," I said.

"We fell asleep watching 'One Piece' last night," Kaitlyn said, grabbing a plate.

"Oh?" her father said. "Well that's nice, you have someone else to watch it with. Angela, help yourself." He motioned to the food—lox, bagels, waffles, bread with butter and jam.

"Thank you," I said appreciative, as my mouth salivated. We sat and ate before heading to school.

CHAPTER EIGHTEEN

Kaitlyn and I talked about so much, and became intimate quickly. In personality, we were starkly different. But in mannerisms and beliefs, we were almost the same person. I found I was more honest with her than I ever was with anyone else. No matter how much time we spent together, I never got tired of her like I did with others. In social settings, the façade I put on would drain my energy, and eventually I would need to go home to recharge my social battery. But with her, I never ran out of energy or natural luster. She put me at ease. I never once pretended to be anything that I was not, or let things that bothered me slide, and I like to think that she did the same with me. We built each other up and felt each other's sadness and happiness. She listened to my meaningless gossip as it turned into existential inquiries.

Our friendship developed so fast, but my love for her was the strongest thing I've ever felt. It wasn't until her that I realized that I never gave much thought to anyone else. I went through the motions of human interaction with no real feeling. Conversations were only a means to an end; I wanted people to think a certain way of me or perform a task. I hated wasting time by talking to someone with no point, only because I didn't know what a meaningful conversation was.

Even to love my parents felt more like an obligation than an affection that I conjured up of my own free will. I'd been born with them; I didn't choose them. As a child, they were wardens to a prison that I was in until I was old enough to make my own decisions. From them, I learned when to say yes or no, and how to keep myself out of trouble. But also with them, I had to stifle a lot of my darker desires. It was always about being proper and being successful. Most of the time I was with them, I had to conceal the truest parts of me just to be respectful to them. They don't even know who I am.

The only friendships I had were with people who ran in my social circle. I had nothing really in common with them, except for our appreciation of name brands. Every relationship I had was more like a business deal. Even Brian I was with only because it made sense on paper. So, having her felt like such a gift.

She opened my eyes to so many things. Or rather, only around her did I feel comfortable enough to acknowledge the world around me and see its truth. I expressed my frustrations with her, which mostly consisted of me complaining at how unfair it was that I had to work twice as hard to be respected.

We shared things with each other that we were unwilling to admit alone. We talked at a low whisper most of the time, so we wouldn't be found and forced out of the comfort of the realm we developed around ourselves. Our inherent shortcomings felt like strengths when we were together. For the first time, I almost felt proud to be what I was. Because if I wasn't, then I wouldn't have her. She was my light in a gray world.

There are things that I regret saying and doing during our time together. Kaitlyn looked at me one day and said, "They don't see us." Very somber. Even out of context, I knew what she meant.

"They don't see *you*," I corrected her.

"No, they don't see you either. They see the money, the things you do for them. The things you're capable of doing. But there's this bubble—"

"Stop." There was a silence while I got my ego under control, so I could calmly say, "you're wrong." At this point I still thought I had everything figured out. I still thought I had control. "It took them a little longer, but eventually I put myself in a position for them to see me. That's why Brian and I have the relationship that we do now." She was reminding me suddenly of my blue-eyed monster. "If you would stop being a weird person, then they would see you too."

And then she became a certain way. Catatonic almost. I would ask her where she goes when she gets that way.

She would say, "I'm just . . . in my head."

This happened a couple of times. Usually when I used sass and brutal honesty to protect my ego. I finally asked her one day what she meant when she said that. I was sitting with her in the shed down the trail from her house. I had just given a crude remark, as was my nature, but instead of retorting back, as was her usual response, she was back in a catatonic state. I urged her to tell me. Back then I never even considered that my words had meaning. It took her a minute to begin. When she did, it was dripping with self-doubt and full of pauses while she gathered herself. I could tell that it was difficult for her to say, and felt flattered that she trusted me enough to try. I have only just started to make sense of the conversation that followed.

"Well I . . . You know how you have subconscious . . . or thoughts that you kind of push to the side because they make you feel a certain way and you can't deal with them right now because you have to function as a person? Well I have to do that a lot to get through my day, because my mind is just a place that I don't want to be in. When I get there, it kind of consumes me. I have to . . . Most of the time I try to stay out of it because it will only make me sad."

"How would you not be in your mind?" I asked. *Are you insane?*

"I just . . . It's like I'm walking on the surface of my own mind." Her eyes searched for words. "Like it's sugar coated. And if the sugar dissolves, I mean if there's a catalyst and something hurts me, in my heart, you know, not some trivial insult, if something hurts my heart and really gets to me then I . . . it's like the sugar dissolves and I fall through . . .

"And it's . . . it's so quick, but I can stop it. I can stop myself falling if I realize that it's happening and I just hold on to the edge, and pull myself back up. And then I'll fortify myself, and stay on the surface. But if I don't stop myself then I fall . . . all the way through."

"What happens if you don't stop yourself? What happens if you fall through?"

This question put some sort of fear into her eyes.

"I just get stuck in there. I start thinking about . . . everything."

In the pause, the wind stopped blowing, and I heard my watch ticking. She continued.

"I get caught up in how . . . I wish that I was a different person so that I could just get through a day with no problem, but I also wish that the people around me were different. I wish other people would realize that life is a joke. Everything that we care about we only do because someone told us we need to. I can't get past how arbitrary everything is, and how some people just land on the more fortunate side of things. I get stuck thinking about all the ways I fall short. And then I sort of spiral, deeper and deeper. And it's hard to climb back to the surface. It takes me a while."

"Well, I don't think you fall short in any way." As she didn't react, I continued to give her countless compliments.

She finally smiled weakly.

She left out the fact that when she spiraled, it was accompanied by a stream of tears. Head banging. The conviction that the only way it could stop was by not existing.

Someone should have been there to help her change the landscape of her mind. Someone should have been around who was capable of showing her her own beauty. I cared about her, but I was still coming out of childhood; I didn't have the right words. If she needed a ladder out of the hole she dug herself into, I could give her one in a heartbeat. But I could only keep her on the surface for so long. She didn't need to cheer up, to get out of her head. She didn't need someone to make her happy, for however long. She needed love herself, to make her mind a better place. She needed to make herself happy. As a high schooler, I didn't understand any of that.

I didn't understand how she could ever feel alone when she had me. Like there was nothing to hold on to. She was so loved. How could that not be enough?

CHAPTER NINETEEN

Friday after school, I ran my errand. I went to Shangri-La, my favorite store for formal clothing. I was picking up the dress I had bought for the dance about a month ago. It wasn't the loveliest when I bought it, but from its original shape, color, and features, I could only see its potential. I had the tailor alter it to fit my desires. I gave my name and order receipt to the attendant and she went in the back to look for it. The tailor came out and asked me how I was doing. I told him I was excited to see the dress again. She came out and handed it to me, pointing me towards the fitting rooms so I could try it on again.

I slipped it on, pulling the straps over my shoulders and moving my body to adjust it so that it was straight. I came out and he helped me up onto a pedestal in front of three panels of mirrors, wrapping around to show my front and both sides. The dress was almost perfect, but not quite as I imagined; the bodice was a little too high.

"Could you lower this neckline?" I asked the tailor. "And hem this up a little higher. I want to be able to see my shoes." Why spend a fortune on them if they're going to be hidden? He drew with chalk where I pointed and stuck pins in to hold the hem until he could get to it with a sewing machine. I went back into the fitting room to take it off and met him back at the counter.

He looked at his calendar or work load or something, and said, "I can have it done by the fifth."

"The *fifth*?" Cutting it close. But I thought about it, and I trusted him, he'd done alterations for many other dresses of mine and never came up short. "Okay, I'll come back then." I began to set a reminder on my phone. "Oh! I

111

won't be able to come that Thursday . . ." I thought about the plausibility of picking it up right before the dance. It would have to work. "I'll pick it up on the sixth."

"The sixth?"

"Yes."

"Okay, no problem. I'll see you then."

I raced back to campus to make the game. It was already crowded. Many alumni came to watch us play our rivals so parking was impossible; I had to park on the other side of campus from the gym. Now I wished I'd stayed at Carol's, instead of going to Shangri-La. I could have left my car parked where it was closer to the gym and dorms, and went to try to pick up my dress over the weekend. Kaitlyn didn't go, and I wished I didn't have to either. I'm sure she thought she had better things to do than cheer with the rest of the student body. I walked into the stadium, which was already packed full. I stepped towards our school's side of the bleachers, scanning for my girls. Searching and searching . . . I finally saw Carol waving at me from the third section. Relieved, I smiled and waved back, heading over. They had just begun the ceremonies. I pushed through the spectators to sit next to Carol, who'd left me a space beside her. The other team, having won last year, went first. Each team honored their seniors and listed their stats and achievements. Carol moved her purse, which she used to mark my spot, and put it on the floor in front of her. Peyton was sitting right behind us, next to Stephanie. She squeezed my shoulder as a hello. I hugged them both in happy reunion. Our head basketball coach started calling our seniors. When he got to Brian, I cheered the loudest. The boys had their medals and certificates, completed the photo op, went straight into the tip off, and the game began.

Sports games were actually the only time at school where I could be unapologetically myself. On game day, we all had one common objective: to win. Everything else faded away. Friend or foe in the hallways, we were all family here in the gym, cheering on our team. We went wild whenever our team scored, did our high school's traditional chants, and gave orders to the referees to favor our team.

Everyone played magnificently, putting their hearts into the game. It was unclear the entire time who would win. We entered the second quarter with our rivals a couple of points in the lead. Brian had the ball! He passed it across the court to a teammate who looked wide open, but number 5 from the other team darted over to intercept the ball.

"Damn!" I exclaimed for him. Number 5 dribbled to the other side of the court, where no one was covering. He did a layup and easily scored a basket. I looked at Brian, he was upset.

Some kid behind me said, "What the hell? He just gave the other team two points!" I turned around.

"Hey, shut up!"

The third quarter began with the rival team ten points ahead, a significant lead but not enough to take us out of the game. The other team had the ball and were dribbling their way down the court. Their strategy was usually short passes all the way down, but number 32 passed across court where there was little coverage. In that pocket, number 26 wasn't being covered, and number 5 eluded his man with his speed. It was unclear who number 32 was throwing to, and both were wide open. They both went for the ball. Number 5 got it, but number 26 was still coming. He ran into his leg and it twisted an unnatural way. Number 5 cried out and tumbled to the ground. The whole crowd went, "Ooh!" in sympathetic pain. We all got quiet as he gritted in pain and the trainers rushed to help him. The team, the coaches, the crowd, everyone took a knee. It tore his ACL. We watched the trainers help him off the court for medical aide and gave an uplifting clap. But he was out of the game. They continued, players refocusing, but you could feel his absence from the way the rival team played.

The score was tied going into the fourth quarter. They went back and forth scoring, so there was no telling who would end up on top. Peyton stuck her head in between me and Carol.

"If we win this game, we're rushing the court!" she said.

We agreed, though I was still expecting the other team to pick up momentum and get ahead again. And sure enough, they scored again shortly after that. Whenever Brian had the ball now, he glided down the court, either passing to assist, or scoring himself.

"Brian is *on* it today!" Carol said after he'd scored again.

"That's my baby!" I was swept up in the excitement of the game.

With seconds on the clock, the other team had the ball. We were ahead only by two points. Number 32 made it down the court and looked for someone to pass to. No one was open. Right before the buzzer went off, number 32 shot a three-pointer, a Hail Mary. The ball hurdled towards the basket. The buzzer sounded just as it hit the backboard . . . and bounced off too much to the right. He missed! We were all up on our feet cheering wildly. That was game! We won this year! We were already moving. In moments, the entire student body was on the court going crazy and celebrating our first win against our rivals in *nine years*! It took a while to get to Brian, my star player. And when I did he lifted me up and spun me around. With all of our friends we just cheered and yelled, I think I saw a couple leaky eyes. True to game day, everything else faded away and we collectively rode the high of a great win.

The excitement died down—only a little. A bunch of us were huddled in a circle right outside the gym, still riding the high.

"I can't believe we won for *our senior year*!" Carol chirped.

"You know we only won because their best player got hurt, right?" Stephanie said.

"I don't care if everyone on the other team was blind. A win is a win," Peyton dismissed her negativity.

The players came out of the locker room and were greeted with another set of cheers and applause from everyone that was outside. Brian came and found our group, receiving high-fives and hugs of congratulations.

"Hey! There's our star player!"

"Great game, bro!"

"You made the last shot. You won us the game!"

He came and stood next to me and held my hand. A boy came up and put a hand on Brian's shoulder. "Hey, when you get drafted in the NBA, let me be your manager, my guy!" Brian laughed.

"Jared, if I make it there, you got it."

"All right! Hey I'm rooting for you man!"

Jared the light-hearted jokester. He was a welcome inconstant member of the group. He could very fluidly travel from friend group to friend group. Racially ambiguous, he claimed to be Black and Korean. He joked about Brian's brief rivalry with number 5.

"When he intercepted the ball, man, the look on your face! You looked like an angry manga character—your eyes just turned into little circles." He imitated the look. I laughed.

"Yeah you could almost see the little red X on his temple!" Jared looked at me surprised, then laughed too because he understood the reference. He had a sidebar with me.

"Yo, Ang, you like anime?

"I love anime!"

"You do?" Brian said.

"Yes! We–I started watching 'One Piece.'"

"Oh, I've heard of that one." Jared said. "I'll have to look at it."

"You can stream it. I'll send you the link."

"Right on! You like Miyazaki films?"

"Of course!" I started singing the Totoro song.

"Aha! That's awesome. Have you seen *Pom Poko*?"

"Mmmm, no I haven't."

"Ah! You have to watch that one, it's my favorite. I have it on DVD I'll lend it to you."

"Okay, thanks!"

Brian watched me have a conversation I never would have had before, seemingly a little uncomfortable. Probably because I was so excitedly talking to another guy.

"Sorry," I said to him. We turned back to the group.

"All right, so let's go celebrate!" Stephanie egged, and that was met by ardent agreement. Brian nudged me.

"Ready, Ang? You want me to drive?" He knew I liked to drink. As fun as that game was, and as excited as I still was for the team, my social battery had run out. All I could think of was getting back to Kait and watching that stupid anime show.

"Actually . . . I think I'm going to head out." Brian looked disappointed. His jubilance instantly faded. "Seriously?" He sighed in frustration, but lightened up a little, "Well, all right, we can go back to my house." He put his arm around me and brushed his face against mine. "We can celebrate on our own."

"Whoops, not what I meant." I slipped out of his embrace. "I'm just really tired. I'm going to go home, by myself."

"Angela . . . we just *won* our *final game*. Are you seriously just going to go home?"

"Aww, Brian!" Jared patted his back. "We'll keep you company tonight, princess." The guys laughed. Brian snorted but I could tell he was pretty embarrassed.

"No, it's not like that!" I tried to help him out. "We had a long night last night and I just need to rest up." I winked at him. They hooted.

"I'll see you later," I said to Brian. He sighed.

"All right. Bye."

And I left to spend the night, and unintentionally the weekend, with my best friend.

I could whittle the saddest parts down to the final two weeks. I think I kicked it off with that simple interaction with Brian. As if it too was in the air, I could feel the change in my life coming. Part of me wanted to stop it and go back to the way things were, back to what I had spent so much time and energy working towards. But the other part of me welcomed it; I secretly wanted it to come. It felt like I was walking into the life that I should have been in all along. I was tired of pushing all of my real feelings away, but I was scared of losing everything. I was terrified. I was letting in all of the things that I had spent so long repressing, and I had no idea what the outcome would be.

CHAPTER TWENTY

Brian came over to my house Monday after school to do homework and spend time with me. On the comfort of my bed, I flipped through the pages of *Pride & Prejudice*, looking for some redeeming quality in Mary, or some tenderness hidden deep in the inner core of Darcy. I lay on my back and looked up at the book in my hands.

"Why is Darcy such an ass?" I asked, sort of rhetorically. Brian didn't respond or make any sort of remark back. I looked over at him. He looked uncomfortable sitting on the edge of my bed with his laptop on his lap, struggling with his English essay.

"Brian?"

"Yeah? Oh, um, I don't know. Crappy childhood, maybe."

I had always marked Darcy's disposition up to him being shy and defensive. Brian's demeanor concerned me. Even when he was working hard, he was always able to joke around with me. I lightly ran my hand down his back. He straightened up.

"Are you all right?" I asked.

After a moment, he seemed to relax. He turned around and took the hand that was on his lower back in his and looked at me. He just looked into my eyes.

"I'm fine," he said. "Sorry, I'm just, um, stressed. I guess."

"Oh. About what?" I squeezed his hand.

He looked at his computer screen. "This essay," he answered. I frowned. He was never worried about school; whatever he lacked academically he made up for on the basketball court. "It's really, um . . . no," he didn't finish. He shook his head. "No, it's not the essay." He sighed and closed the computer and set it on the bed. He grabbed my hand again in both of his. He wanted to say something, but he was struggling for the words to say it. He really was torn.

I sat up. "What's wrong?"

He closed his eyes. When he opened them again they were hard and concentrated on mine. "You have to stop hanging out with her."

I knew who he was talking about. I smiled. "What? Brian, don't worry about it. Is it about what everyone thinks of her? Because she's actually pretty awesome." I moved myself to be more upright. "Brian, you've developed so much rancor for her, you've *got* to let go of it. It's just not healthy. If you actually got to know her—"

"No," he cut me off. "Stop hanging out with her. It's changing you."

"Changing me?" I'm less shallow. "I don't talk to her during school since I know you guys still don't like her. I don't even acknowledge her because you made it clear you'd be embarrassed if people knew we were friends. But I don't see how it's a problem if we spend time together after school."

"I mean, I haven't seen you all weekend. You've been ditching me and all of your friends to be with *her*. You even want to go to the dance with her, as a double date thing. Is it about what we did? Are you trying to make it up to her or something? Because you don't have to. You don't have to feel guilty, Angie. It was so long ago and you did nothing wrong."

"What is wrong with me hanging out with her?"

"People are starting not to like you."

I furrowed my eyebrows. "That's not true," I said.

He snickered sarcastically. "Yeah, it is. People are starting to talk about you. Not good stuff."

"Then defend me." Then he got serious and looked down. I put a hand on his arm. "You're my boyfriend. Part of the relationship is that we have each other's backs. I know this is difficult to understand but I would really appreciate it if you would just support me. What happened to 'any adventure'?"

"This isn't an adventure, Angela. This is some charity case that's gone too far." He sighed and put his hands together, elbows on his knees. "I can't hang out with you anymore."

"What?" I looked at him for a while incredulously. He just kept looking at his hands. Then I laughed. Of course, he had to be kidding. "Yes, you can, stop being stupid. You really worried me for a second." I relaxed a little and sat back. "So Richard is getting the limo for the dance. Oh, and you need to wear a red tie because my dress is—" He got frustrated and abruptly turned to me.

"I'm not being stupid. I just . . . I don't want to be in the same boat as you. I can't . . . I went completely out of my comfort zone to be with you in the first place, and now you're spending all this time with this girl as if . . ." he was really struggling with his words. Or maybe he was dancing around something. "I mean, are you really willing to ruin everything? You're lucky I even started talking to you."

"What are you talking about? People love me. You love me," I guess he didn't hear that last part because he was already talking over me.

"People love what you can do for them. They love the power you can have, despite who you are. You especially should be happy to have what you do. Wealthy family, great friends, *me* . . . And now you're ruining it, and you're going to regret it. What are you going to do when you're on your own? Do you think people will still respect you when you don't have an in?" Then I realized what he was talking about. I looked down at my hands. *Despite who I was.* I realized that although my experiment had taken an unexpected turn, I had gotten my answer.

"She's crazy, Angie. Don't you see that? She's going to bring you down to her level." Tears started to fill up in my eyes. "If you stop talking to her, I might take you back. But if not . . ."

That was quite the ultimatum. "Get out, please." I whispered.

"Look, I'm sorry, but—"

I didn't let him finish. I jumped up and grabbed his computer off the bed. I put it in his bag and shoved the bag into his chest. He grunted from the force. He zipped it up quietly and slung it over his shoulder as he stood up.

"Ang—" he started. I pushed him as hard as I could towards the door. "Get out!" I yelled at him, pointing to the door. He looked shocked. "Get out of my house!"

"All right, look . . ." I went over and picked up the snow globe he got me off my bedside table and threw it at him. He dodged it and it shattered as it hit the wall.

"Leave!" Tears were pouring down my face. He took a step backwards towards the door then paused. He hesitated there for a minute, trying to think of something to say. He started to say my name again.

"No," I said with weight, as if that was the end to it all. He shook his head at me, then turned around and left. I stood there for a moment in desolation. The water from the snow globe trickled down the wall. I watched it make a spider web design, as my heart pounded in my throat.

I walked to my dresser and looked in the mirror on top of it. I had always thought of myself as just pretty. But now I started to see myself in a completely different way, and I couldn't stop it.

I drove to her house, choking back tears all the way. She was not at home. Her mom said she hadn't seen her since she left for school that morning. I walked the trail and found her in the shed. "Brian . . ." I started, but I couldn't finish. I just shook my head and sat down on the ground. I put my head on my knees and cried.

She sat down next to me and held me. After a while of listening to me cry, she said, "I never really liked that guy. Just kinda looks funny, you know?'

I laughed. I appreciated her automatically being on my side. I told her he broke up with me, and I told her why—the real reason. I told her our whole conversation. After I was finished we sat in silence. She said nothing. Suddenly I felt awkward, like maybe I had overestimated our friendship and I had just brought on way too much for her. I thought maybe I had hurt her feelings by telling her what Brian had said. I turned my head towards her and saw that she was crying, too. Then I started to say I was sorry, but she cut me off by hugging me. Then I let go. Something clicked and I just felt like it was okay to be sad. I sobbed on her shoulder. I cried and cried and cried. And she was there for me the whole time.

"You didn't love him, did you?" I looked at her, into those eyes I couldn't help but be honest to.

"No, no I didn't. I guess I was in love with . . . what he gave me. I've been so obsessed with being well-liked." And then what my mother said earlier sank in. "I've been so obsessed with power and affiliation, and controlling everyone else . . . I never really cared about any of them."

She sighed. "You really are awful. But you know Brian breaking up with you isn't your fault, right?" She paused as she gathered the pieces of her story. "There's a bubble—"

"I know," I stopped her. I'd heard this too many times. And I wasn't ready yet to let it sink in.

I sat up; I knew I had to say something. "Kaitlyn. I'm so sorry."

She chuckled. "Why are *you* sorry?"

"No, I mean . . . in the seventh grade," I looked down at my hands. I had to start over. "In the seventh grade I said something—"

"About my parents being drug dealers?" She interrupted me with a straight face. I nodded cautiously. I didn't know she knew it was me.

"Oh, it's all right." She was brushing it off.

I shook my head, "No it's not all right. You were so upset and I—"

"Hey," she cut me off again. "That's not why I was upset. Not because of some stupid rumor. I'd heard so many of those," she said with a smile. "My dad always said that our wealth probably 'intimidated' people." She shrugged. I got a pang of jealousy. "I was used to that, or whatever it was. I just . . . I hated having to go through it on my own. I had no one at school to stand by me, or even believe in me or my family. Eventually, I think I believed it myself. Not, of course, that my parents were drug dealers," she shot a glare at me. I bit my lip. She sighed, "For the first time I actually believed that there was something wrong with me. Something sinister or dishonest. Something attributable . . . to my appearance. And then, I don't know, something changed inside of me. I kind of lost faith and interest in everyone around me. I lost my ignorance and bliss, and I couldn't bring it back. And I have tried. It just felt *better* to be on my own. That's why . . . that night. I wasn't surprised. It broke my heart, but, I knew why."

I understood. I had done whatever I could to keep myself on top, worked twice as hard for my praise. She did the opposite. She kept herself down so she didn't have to feel the burn of everyone else's judgment. She voluntarily stayed in the mud just so she couldn't be pushed back down into it. But that just made people gain more distaste for her.

I wrapped my arms around her and rested my head on her shoulder. Without the prejudice of my friends, or the stereotypes of the outside world around us, I felt the connection that we shared. I felt the equality that existed due to our human limitations. I felt our true friendship stem from mutual understanding. And for the first time, I felt whole.

"Hey, Kait?"

"Yea?"

I paused. The gravity of what I had to say made me feel so weak, but so sure at the same time.

"We . . . I should have saved you."

Seconds of stillness followed.

"I know," she said. She heard my apology. "Let's not talk about it."

We sat in silence for the rest of the night, listening to the world. She rested her cheek on my forehead, and after a while, our heartbeats matched up. We were in harmony; in sync with each other, and the sounds of the night.

◊

We arrived around 10 o'clock at night. Johnny wasn't quite old enough to drive, but of course he did. We parked at the foot of the trail—about a quarter mile from the shed. We all stood behind his car, as he handed out items from his trunk.

A car pulled up behind us. "Who is that?" I whispered to Brian, jerking my chin at the boy who climbed out. He held an unlit cigarette between his lips, as he came towards us. He leaned against Johnny's car and pulled out a lighter.

"Matt, Johnny's partner in crime," he smiled at me, nudging my side. "Like us." He didn't ease my worry. "I've met him, he's cool. He's fun like Johnny, but he's more, uh . . . sensible. He'll keep him in line." He winked at me.

I felt something cold and heavy being pressed against my arm. I turned to Annette handing me a sledgehammer, a wide smile stamped across her face.

"Oh, no. I can't." I refused. "I'm just going to watch you guys." I took a step back. Johnny came around and got in my face.

"No watching. You're either here to join the party or you leave." Brian's hand flashed in front of me and then he was standing between us. He didn't say anything, but Johnny seemed to get the idea of the glare. He snarled and continued rummaging through his trunk. Brian turned to face me, and took the sledgehammer from Annette.

He took my hand. "If you're uncomfortable, we can leave. But you don't have to worry. I'm right here. I really want you to have fun tonight. It's just a wooden shed, Angie. Relax," he put the tool in the hand that he held and wrapped my fingers around it. "Do it for me." He gave me a squinty eye smile.

I nodded. "Okay."

We all walked the distance to the little wooden shed. I was walking next to Brian, holding his hand. Matt saddled up to walk on the other side of me.

"So, you lose a bet?" he asked, talking around his cigarette.

"What?"

"How'd they talk you into coming along tonight?" I didn't answer, just stared at him. "It's just that I've never seen you before, and now you're tagging along on one of Johnny's pleads for jail time. So I assume you either lost a bet, or you're just reckless. And you trying to refuse to participate tells me that you're not reckless. So what was the bet?"

"Oh, no I just, I'm not that handy with a tool, and I didn't want to slow the whole operation down. I want to be here. I didn't lose a bet."

"Oh," he said playfully, lifting his eyebrows. I was starting to get irritated; I didn't think I liked the implication of his words. "It's a lot to risk for a night of teenage rebellion. I mean, if I hadn't known this guy since third grade, I wouldn't be hanging out with him, especially not at night. Are you sure you want to be here for this?"

"We're just doing some damage, and then getting out of there. It's not that much of a risk."

He peered at me sideways. "Who are you here for?"

I paused. "I'm here for myself. Can you leave me alone?"

"No, tell me really. Who are you doing this for? Who do you want to see you?"

I growled, "I'm not here for anyone, I'm here because I want to be. They wanted me here and I came because they're my friends."

He smiled wide at that last word. His cigarette was nothing but filter now, and he flicked it onto the ground in front of him, stomping it out as he walked past it. "So you're just living out a fantasy, huh?" he said, lighting another one. The sly look on his face made me so mad.

We finally approached the shed, entering into a clearing. I steered Brian to the left to get away from Matt. We all stood in front of it, taking it in for a second. The boys were making jokes, and Annette hung on Johnny's arm. He shrugged her off and walked to the side of the shed closest to us.

"Let's do this."

The first strike was the loudest. The shock of it ran down my spine, taking all of my worry and making it real with a sense of alarm. The bat that Johnny used had spikes at the end, which tore through the wood. It had to be ripped out with a loud splintering sound in order to be recovered. Johnny had a maniacal look on his face, looking satisfied with his swing, eager for more destruction. The strike seemed to shock him too for a second; he had to take a step back to gather himself again. With the bat in his hand, he looked at each of us.

"Come on now, guys! Don't leave it all to me!" With an eerie laugh, he struck again, and another blunt bang broke the stillness of the night. Then more bangs, more rapidly, as others started to join in. Brian, standing next to me, squeezed my hand. I met his eyes, and we communicated that way for a second. Then I pulled my hand away.

I walked towards the south wall of the shed, weapon in hand. My worry was that we would be caught, and charged with destruction of private property. Or that someone would lose control and, if we were standing too close to one another, injure someone else. More, I worried that we were the type of people to destroy things—that I was working to make friends with people who caused trouble just for the sake of it. I couldn't take the time to think about it anymore; I wanted to keep Brian, more than anything. And to keep him, I had to do what certain people asked of me. So I swung. And it was the second most unsettling sound of that night. All of my worry seemed to be in that one action, disappearing in the thickness of the wood. I exhaled; I had been holding my breath for a while. I looked around to see if anyone else was as affected by the action as I was. However, all of my accomplices were engrossed in their own tasks: punching holes in walls, breaking apart wood, claiming their status in the teenage kingdom of bad decisions. I swung again.

I felt like my soul had so much to work out, and it all faded with every beat of my heart. I did lose myself in the destruction. I was having fun. I felt invigorated with the crude tool in my hands, using all of my strength in every swing. I laughed out loud, head back, looking towards the beautiful night sky.

Then I smelled something strong and heard a sprinkling, and whipped around to find the source. It came from inside the shed. I walked to the doorway and looked in. Johnny was emptying a can around the room.

"What are you doing!?" I yelled.

"Shhh," he continued sprinkling the gasoline. He chuckled, "Can't leave any fingerprints."

I gave him a shove. "Are you crazy? We can't do that. This is—"

"Chill out, Ang," Brian cut me off as he walked over. "Johnny, it's wood. There are no fingerprints. Where did you even get that?"

Matt interjected, "You're gonna set us all on fire, dumbass." That cigarette never left his lips.

"It was in the back. This is the same as what we're already doing." His eyes became wicked. "But now we get to have some real fun. Don't tell me you don't want to see this place lit up. You like art, Angie. Think of how beautiful a fire would look against the night sky," he taunted me. Annette came up and put her arm around me.

"Yes! Let's watch it burn!" she exclaimed.

I guess we were too busy arguing to hear a third girl coming up behind us. "What are you guys doing?" We all turned around. She was in boys' shorts and a tee shirt that said PINK across the front.

"Kaitlyn . . ." I whispered, dumbfounded.

She looked at Johnny holding the can, and looked around at the damage we had already done. She shook her head in disgust and began to walk away. As she did, she pulled out a cell phone from the pocket of her shorts. Johnny lurched after her, dropping the can, letting it splash out.

"Hey! What are you going to do with that?" He made an attempt to take it from her. She jerked away and slapped the hand that reached for her. This just made Johnny angrier. For all of his cleverness, he didn't see the value in keeping his cool in this moment. He grabbed her arm and covered her mouth and dragged her deeper into the shed with him. We all followed, yelling at Johnny to calm down, telling Kaitlyn to put her phone down, trying to pull them away from each other.

Matt took her other arm and tried to talk to her to calm her down, talking around lit paper. But, with both of her arms being held, she kicked Matt in the shin. He exclaimed and limped to lean against the doorway. With her now free hand, Kaitlyn slapped Johnny in the face.

Johnny shoved her into a wall, and she slumped against it. When she hit it, there was an awful thudding sound, and then a creaking that never stopped. Everything seemed to pause. Everyone's eyes widened, while our bodies froze. We heard the creak start when her head hit the wall, and it seemed to travel, up and across the walls and the roof. Then, there was a final breaking sound, and everything sped up. We had the sense to run out of the wooden structure before it all came down.

We were out of the door, out of the shed, but when the roof came down, it and the front-facing wall fell forward. I got knocked to the ground. In trying to get up I had to shove a wooden panel off of me. It gave me a splinter and I thought that was an awful pain. Matt was beside me and helped me the rest of the way up. There was nothing between his lips. Johnny was dusting himself off. I found Brian on the ground groaning next to him. I helped him up, asking if he was all right.

"Yeah, I'm fine. I just hit my head." He stretched his neck, cocking his head to the side and holding his right temple. Then his body stiffened. His eyes looked down, and seemed to focus on something far away. He suddenly picked his head up. "What does it smell like?" he asked me.

I breathed in through my nose. And then everything lit up. So quickly, there was fire everywhere. It started ten feet from us, and rushed towards the back of the rubble of wood, spreading everywhere that Johnny had sprinkled the gasoline. Smoke rose up to block the stars. It got so hot I had to lift my arm up to block my face.

There was a wail, and we looked to see Annette on her stomach under two large panels of wood, unable to get up or move. Then we heard police sirens approaching.

"We have to go!" yelled Matt.

"I know, I know," Johnny stood there. He appeared to be deliberating.

"HELP ME!" screamed Annette, eyes widened.

Johnny cursed under his breath. "All right, all right! Grab that end, we have to lift this." We all grabbed a side to lift, and Annette was able to squeeze out. The sirens came closer. She took off running as soon as she could get up. Johnny and Matt followed. Brian started.

"Wait!" I yelled. Kaitlyn still lay unconscious, under the rafters that pinned her down. I moved towards her.

"What are you doing?" Brian yelled, grabbing my arm.

"We have to help her!" I said frantically. Brian looked at me incredulously.

"What? No!" he said. "We have to go, Angie!"

"She won't be able to get out!"

"It doesn't matter, Angie! It doesn't matter!"

He pulled me away, and I pulled back.

"We're not leaving her here, Brian."

He moved close to me. "Get it together, Angie. Don't risk getting caught for *her*!" I felt threatened.

I looked back. She was waking up. She looked around groggily, and realized she was pinned under the roofing, as the fire blazed closer to her. The look of horror on her face has been seared into my mind since that night. She started to twist and wriggle, but could not budge. With every little move she made, blood gushed out around where wood stuck into her thigh. The rafter that held her down at one end remained propped up on the opposite wall at the other, too heavy to move. Another log nailed to it made a cross, and lay across her diagonally, immobilizing her, digging into her shins.

She looked up and saw us. She reached out, whimpering, pleading with the little energy she had left to use. The sirens were blaring.

"We don't have time!" He tugged on me again. My eyes welled, as my horror matched hers. I turned away, and followed Brian, running close behind him deeper into the woods. We made a wide arc back to the cars, away from the direction the sirens were coming from.

The last thing I saw of the scene was of her trying to crawl away, the weight of the roof pinning her down. We just left her there, like she was nothing. We approached the car and I got in the backseat next to Brian. Before I got the door closed, I heard a scream pierce through the night.

CHAPTER TWENTY-ONE

My eyes flew open. The sun stung them, intensified as it reflected off of my gold walls, and I cringed. I lay trying to get myself together for the next couple of minutes, listening to the ticking of my watch. I didn't look at it. It was a school day, but if I was late, I didn't care.

Sure enough, I heard my mom call up to me. I stayed quiet and sat still, waiting for her to huff and puff down the hallway and come into my room. The footsteps, the loud, hurried knocks, and there she was.

"Angie! You're late, get up!" I stared at her for a bit, until her face morphed and her tone softened a little. "Are you okay?"

"Mama, will you sit on my feet?"

She cocked her head to the side and peered at me. "You're not going today, are you?" I shrugged. She sighed, then reached down and felt around for my toes. When she found them, she gave them a little squeeze, and then sat down on top of them, anchoring me down. It made me feel tethered down—secure; I wasn't going to float off anywhere. As long as she stayed on my feet, I stayed grounded and close to her, and nothing in the moment could ever change.

She rested her arm on my bent knees and looked at me. "What's wrong?"

"Nothing," I said with emotion. "I just don't want to see anyone right now."

"I hear that." She shifted, moving to lean against the wall. "My daughter, who loves you?" she asked, beginning a mantra that was as old as I was. I smiled.

"You," I responded.

"What are you going to do?"

I wiggled my toes. "Be strong for you," I answered. It was a call and response we did when I was very little. Sometimes just because, but especially when I was upset from a fall. It brought back memories of watching her pour evil witch hazel on my wounds, and them not hurting as bad because of her magical spell.

She added something this time, "You're already strong. Now you just have to be good."

In the comfort of her warmth and stability, I said, "I know."

After a couple more hours of lounging, I got dressed to make it to school in time for lunch.

I waited by the door at the north end of the dining hall. She entered this way every day, because her last class before lunch was down the hall from where I stood. In a moment, the floor flooded with high school students, looking for meat. Many made their way around me, and I waited patiently, my heart expressing my emotions for me. Finally, I saw her walking down the hall toward me. She walked at a glacial pace, but it felt like she was in front of me in an instant. I think she sensed that she was the one I was looking for. I held out my hand and she slowly put hers in mine, making her eyes into slits.

"Will you eat with me?" Her eyebrows scrunched together now, and then she smiled. I felt her fingers relax around mine and I gave them a squeeze. This was the first time I acknowledged her as a friend at school. I led her, hand in hand, into the dining hall. I knew people paused and looked at us, but I pretended not to notice. We grabbed food and sat at her normal table. On the way over, I passed the table my friends sat at. Carol and Peyton looked on in confusion. Anna did an unimpressive job of hiding her amusement. Richard looked pleased, perhaps with himself. He winked at me. Brian sat at the end of the table. He made an effort not to look up. If he did, I don't know whether or not my resolve would have changed in that moment.

We sat down and ate lunch at a new table, and acted as if we were alone— just pleased with our conversation, sharing laughs, discussing classes we hated and teachers we loved. I had never done anything outside of what was popular. It was a chore for me to keep up a certain appearance, and maintain my aura of importance. Every day in school was an opportunity to show that I let nothing hold me back, and to let everyone know that any stereotype they could conjure up based on my color didn't apply to me. But all that did was make them think that I did not identify with my physical features. I should have made them stop with the stereotypes. On top of that, I made sure that others like me stayed down, so that I could climb on top. I used the disadvantage that we all had to work in my favor, by making an alliance with others and letting them know that I agreed with them. In disparaging them, I did nothing to exalt my sisters, and for once, I felt shame in doing that. For once, I wanted to show that I stood with my kind, my color, my kin.

Stereotyping and discrimination will never stop, and I will never outrun my features, but we can work to change the image that has been perpetuated. Instead of not identifying with my color, I should have been letting people know what group I am a part of, and showing them who we are. We will show them a better face—the right face. We will create our own image, and erase the damage that has been done to us.

I got so lost in my determination that I neglected to acknowledge how impossible of a feat this would be to accomplish. I wish we could have just been happy with what we had: knowing that, if all else failed, we still had each other.

"Hey, Angela." Jared had appeared, handing something to me across the table. "Here you go!" I took it and read the front.

"Oh! Thank you!"

"No problem! You can just bring it back when you're done." He waved and went back to his own table.

"What is that?" Kaitlyn asked, looking at the DVD.

"It's *Pom Poko*. He said I could borrow it to watch."

"Oh, I haven't seen that one."

"We can watch it tonight."

"Okay. Cool! See," she shook my arm. "aren't you glad I introduced you to Miyazaki?"

"Yes," I said bitingly, giving her the satisfaction.

We continued to talk until the lunch period ended, and we parted ways to go to our classes.

I felt invigorated by how well that day went for us. I didn't feel threatened or worried about the eyes on me. I felt proud of myself for being brave, untouchable because I had a shield of importance around me. Being with her was easier than being with anyone else. I didn't have to pretend to be anything to impress her or push away my feelings to seem too uninterested to be bothered. I didn't have to put on *any* sort of act for her; I knew she would love me regardless. And I didn't worry about what anyone else thought. Carol and Peyton didn't reach out to me to question me, either because they were too afraid to or didn't care, but that was okay. This was the feeling of home and security that I had been looking for but could never reach. She was my happiness—a reflection of all the parts of me that I liked and even more that I lacked. I cared for her in ways that I didn't even know I could and doubt I ever will again. I think back to the first real conversation we had at that Peruvian restaurant with Richard. I thought that power was the basic commodity that would satisfy me, because that's what I'd used to win people over. Richard thought it was money, because his white privilege told him that that was all he needed; society would take care of the rest. But Kaitlyn, who could see more than any of us, knew that it was freedom. Freedom is the most basic necessity that humans crave. And she gave me that. Through our friendship, she gave me the freedom to be who I was, without regret. And I was grateful.

CHAPTER TWENTY-TWO

Having spent the day much the same as the day before, Anna caught up with me after school as I waited for the activities committee meeting to start. I was outside the door waiting for Kaitlyn, scrolling through social media apps on my phone. When I heard footsteps at the other end of the hall, naturally I glanced up to see who it was, and once Anna's face accosted my eye sockets I looked back down and resumed my scrolling, paying no more attention to the world outside of my screen. But as those footsteps came sauntering down the hall, I realized that they only had one destination. I looked up as she stepped up to me and put my phone back in my pocket so I could do her the favor of giving her all my attention. We then engaged in a nice conversation.

"Hey, Angie."

"Hey, Anna." All smiles. "How's your week going?"

"It's so great. How is the single life treating you?" She put on a little pout. "Not too lonely I hope, after Brian dumped you." Once Carol and Peyton arrived, they stood by us to listen to the conversation.

"No, I'm actually doing just fine, thanks for asking," I said pleasantly.

"Oh, that's right! You have someone to fill the void, don't you? Kelly, is it?"

"Yea, close enough."

"I'm surprised it took Brian that long to realize that you were so far beneath him. You guys were hard to watch, he was so out of your league. We're all glad he finally came to his senses. But no worries, I'm keeping him company now. I'll make sure he doesn't make the same mistake again."

She winked at me as she said "keeping him company." As Anna and I conversed, Carol and Peyton took on the role of wallflowers. It slightly amused me how they allowed me and Anna to continue with no objections. Anna and I had never been close. We were rarely civil.

"Oh good. I am kind of surprised that you had to wait until I had my go with him before you could. But I'm so glad you're not above taking leftovers. If you want to know what he likes in bed, feel free to ask."

She didn't have anything to say to that.

"I also wanted to let you know," she looked around, eyes landing on Carol and Peyton for backup. "Since you've decided to associate yourself with people even less reputable than *you*, we no longer want your company. So even when you realize how worthless you are, don't try to come back to our group. We do not consider you a friend." I knew she was speaking for everyone by the way Carol and Peyton shuffled and looked down.

In all this time, no one had reached out to me. No one had even looked my way except to glance at what they could not believe. But here the three of them stood, answering the question that I had completely forgotten I had asked. There it was, so simple and obvious and yet so devastating. Although I had gathered the answer on my own, to have it confirmed, to have it said out loud, still broke my heart. I can honestly say it didn't break because I was looking to these people for approval. It did because I knew I had so much to offer that would never shine through. These people to me represented the greater whole of who they were. They represented a structure that I would never be able to break down. They represented a life of cool indifference that I would never know, sponsored by a safety net that I would never have. They represented the privilege that I so ignorantly thought I was a part of for the majority of my life. Realizing now that that couldn't be further from the truth paralyzed me for a moment. I almost faltered. But then the moment was over and I came back. I came back to loving who I was, who I had around me, who truly supported me. I offered nothing to these people in front of me if I wasn't buying things or giving myself to them. They didn't value me as a person. And I didn't care to be anywhere near that.

Out of the corner of my eye, I saw Kaitlyn come around the corner of the hallway. I smiled. I looked Anna in the eyes and I said, "That's all right with me."

And I think that my sincerity bothered her because she didn't seem satisfied with her mission.

Kaitlyn approached me, looking a bit cautious and confused. I took her hand to lead her into the meeting room, telling her, "We were just wasting time."

I walked in with Kaitlyn, brushing past the former members of my trio. That was the last time I was in the presence of those friends that I had had for years. I don't know if they would have welcomed me back but I never looked for their friendship or validation again. No more masks, no more lingering questions. This one person offered me more strength than those two combined.

I wasn't ready to do homework, so after the meeting I followed her back to her house and laid on the lounger in her bedroom, daydreaming.

"The dance is coming together really well." I said. "I'm surprised that our little club did such a good job planning."

She moaned in agreement from the bed.

"Aren't you excited?"

She crooked her neck to look over at me. "Are you going?"

I was astounded at this question. "Of course I'm going! How could I not? We spent so much time on it, and it's going to be the best one our school has ever had."

"Oh, because you're planning it?"

"Of course, because I'm planning it. And it's going to kick off spring break so everyone will have time to marinate on the fact that *I* made it perfect."

"Yes, all you," she chuckled. "I just thought, since you and Brian broke up, you wouldn't want to go."

"That's ridiculous. Of course I still want to go. I'll just keep myself busy, checking on everything, making sure everything goes smoothly. Plus, I'm not leaving you and Richard alone together."

"Wow you're annoying. So, I guess I have to find a dress."

I sat completely up. "You don't have one yet?"

She shrank away from me like she was in trouble. "No . . ." she answered slowly. "And I wasn't going to get one since I thought you weren't going. Are you sure your ego isn't going to be too damaged walking in there alone?"

"Shut up. We need to go shopping this weekend! Open up your laptop, we can look at dresses online."

She moved slowly. "Do we have to? I'm sure I can find one to wear in my closet." I gasped.

"Wear a dress you've already worn?"

"I'm sure I haven't worn all of—"

"Absolutely not!" I yanked open her laptop when she finally brought it over at the pace of a sloth. "It's so late! What if you have to get it taken up or something?" I gasped again. "And Richard needs to know what color tie to get to match! Why would you wait this long?"

She stuck her tongue out at me. "Look!" She pointed at the curtains blocking out the sun in her window. "Those are a nice pattern. Are you handy with a sewing machine?"

"This is serious, Katie Scarlett."

"Oh," she mocked me. "I'm so sorry. In that case, the couch in the living room downstairs has much better fabric and design."

I sneered. "I will honestly rip up your couch if that's what it takes."

CHAPTER TWENTY-THREE

Much to her dismay and eventual acceptance, we spent the majority of our Saturday shopping for the perfect dress to no avail. After our spree, I drove us back to my house from the mall.

"We'll have better luck tomorrow," I said. "It takes patience to find the perfect dress."

"We found about five perfect dresses. Just not 'Angela' perfect."

"We found all mediocre dresses, and zero 'Kaitlyn' dresses."

"I just don't look good in anything. I might as well go in a potato sack."

"No," I said sharply. "You just need a dress that highlights all of your pretty features and . . . hides the bad. It's hard to get a dress that does both." She didn't say anything.

The real problem was that all the dresses we looked at just drew attention to her lacerations. She had a great body but most of it was covered in them. The backseat was full of shopping bags, most of them mine, none of them containing any ball gowns. Kaitlyn reached in a bag of leftovers from our lunch at the food court and pulled out a homemade-looking bottle of liquid that was green with little specks in it. It looked like vomit.

"Where did you get that?" I asked.

"I got it from that tea shop next to the Victoria's Secret."

Ah. I had been too preoccupied shopping in the place that mattered.

"And what is it?" I asked skeptically, watching the specks slosh around in the liquid.

"It's tea. Chupacabra tea." I'm sure that's not what she said, but that's what I remember hearing. I looked at it with disgust. She continued.

"It's supposed to be really healthy, and good for your digestive system. It's got live organisms in it, and chia seeds." That part I no doubt heard and remember correctly.

"What the hell? Don't drink that, throw it away. It sounds like they tricked you."

"No, it's good. I've had it before. It's kind of an acquired taste but you'll love it once you try it."

As she said this she started to open it up, and it started fizzing like a carbonated drink. I heard the angry hissing sound and worried for my seats.

"Careful! Don't let it spill."

I looked over and she continued to open it and the fizzing continued, and I saw the foam rising to the top.

"It's going to overflow, stop opening it."

"I'm doing it slowly; it'll stop once I relieve some pressure."

But it didn't stop fizzing. In fact, the more she opened it, the stronger the fizzing became. It quickly became a tea bomb, spraying organisms all over my car.

"Kaitlyn!"

"I don't know why it's doing this!"

"Close it!"

"No, it'll stop!"

My eyes went back and forth from the road to the spray of vomit.

"Throw it out, throw it out the window!"

My fingers fumbled on the side of my door looking for the window button.

"I'm closing it, I'm just gonna close it!"

She fumbled with the bottle cap and dropped it. I couldn't find the button for the window, so I swung over two lanes to pull over onto the shoulder so she could open her door and throw it out, but as the car swung, so did the drink. It slopped all over me and my center console. I shrieked. She gasped.

I was finally pulled over onto the shoulder just as it stopped exploding, organisms spewed all over my seats, the roof, and our clothes. We just sat there looking around at the mess for a second in silence. I looked at her, and she looked back with a very guilty look on her face. I reached to my left side and unlocked the car doors.

"Get out," I said.

She smiled and extended her arm out towards me.

"You might as well try it now," she said. She had ruined the seats in my car—I had to get them refurbished to get rid of the smell, and yet she sat there smiling. I loved her smile.

CHAPTER TWENTY-FOUR

I eventually forgave her, and we set out again on Sunday, in her car, to the few stores within a twenty-mile radius that we hadn't tried the day before. In the last store, looking at the last dress she tried on, we both felt defeated. She stepped out of the fitting room and stood in front of the mirror. I pulled my bottom lip to the side in pain.

She sighed. "I'm surprised you're still here."

"Of course," I said. "We'll find the one for you eventually."

She turned towards me and got silent. A question seemed to be forming in her mind, an aura of distress coming over her. I thought it was about the dress. I stepped towards her and hurriedly said, "Don't worry. We'll look somewhere else. This is hardly the last stop," as I waved my hands to the sides in an arc, as if making the problem disappear with the simple movement.

She shook herself back to reality. "What? Oh, yeah okay. I'm going to go take this off." And she disappeared back into the fitting room. I plopped down on the loveseat placed for people waiting for the fitting rooms. I couldn't let another day end with us unsuccessful in our goal. I thought, and a solution I wanted to disregard crept into my mind. She came out of the dressing room, a question still lingering on her face. I sighed.

"Come on," I motioned her.

"Ang," she said, fatigued. "I will just wear something in my closet, this is too much now."

"Come on, Kait, we will try one more place and then I'll let it go. I'll drive."

Begrudgingly, I took her to the last place I knew with gorgeous formal wear—the boutique that had humiliated me. Obviously, I hadn't been back since then and I never intended to go back, but I wanted so badly to find her the perfect dress. Maybe I thought this would make up for everything.

When I pulled up at the mall, she said, "We've been to every store here already."

"Not every store. There's one more we didn't go to." I found a spot to park and we got out of the car.

"Did you forget about it yesterday?"

"No, last time I was here they were very rude to me so I didn't want to go back."

She snorted; this amused her. "Were they actually rude or did they not cater to your highness?"

"Excuse me what is *that* supposed to mean? They were *actually rude*. I have a very valid reason to complain. They should be ashamed of themselves."

"Okay, calm down. All I'm saying is, sometimes you can be a little entitled." My mouth opened. "Okay," she continued when I couldn't say anything. "I'm sorry, I'm sure you had a valid reason not to go back."

"No . . ." I said after a beat. "I can be a little entitled. And maybe I did overreact a little." Slamming my hand on the counter came to mind. "But I honestly think they were out of line."

"So why did you change your mind on coming back?" I looked at her fondly. I wrapped my arm around her as we started walking in.

"You're worth it."

"Aww." She wrapped hers around me.

"Plus, now that I have my wallet on me I want to prove I can afford everything."

"*That* sounds more like you."

I led her to the boutique, expecting to confront my arch nemeses. But none of the same employees were even working that day. We started looking at the selection of dresses. We looked around with purpose. An employee offered to help and I respectfully declined. We'd been through this enough times to know we didn't need to waste anyone else's time along with us.

"How about this one?" Kaitlyn said. And I turned around already expecting to be unimpressed with whatever garbage bag she held up. But there it was. The dress that had gotten me run out of the store. I was so stupefied I laughed.

"What?"

"Nothing." I moved to her, feeling the dress again, picturing it on her. Having a small frame and a small chest, the shape would look elegant on her. And the cutouts on the sides were placed exactly where they needed to be from what I could remember of the placement of her marks. And those gems, even more majestic than I remembered. I nodded. "Yes! Go try it on." We had also done this enough times to know that dresses look far different worn than on the rack.

She walked in the fitting room and I sat on the chair outside. I prayed this was the one. The dance was so close and I didn't have the energy either to continue the search. Though I had to admit, I loved just being with her. I would have gone to a thousand stores if it meant more time with her.

I heard the curtain rings slide on the railing. She walked out of the fitting room, curtain swinging shut behind her. My breath caught. Stunning. Just as I wanted for her, it displayed her assets without showing the flaws. The charmeuse fabric clung to her curves, flaunting how skinny she was. The deep V neckline featured her bosom without appearing vulgar or tacky. Indeed, she was graceful and sophisticated.

I was so excited I hugged her, giving her the same energy she gave me that night after dinner with Richard. I felt like a proud mom.

"Perfect." She smiled and looked down.

"Great. Can we go home now?"

"Yes. After many, many pictures." I pulled my phone out. "Smile!"

That night we half-heartedly did homework in her room. I sat at her desk and she sat on the bed, with the appearance of being studious. We read directions over and over again as we lost focus halfway through the sentences. Flipped pages and made irrelevant conversation. We had just finished talking about history—a subject she was far more knowledgeable about and interested in than I was, when she started an irrelevant conversation that threw me completely.

With a thought on her face, she said, "Angie?"

"Yeah?" I replied, not understanding why she had to call for my attention when we were just talking. She seemed to be straining herself trying to continue.

"What made you go to the shed that night? I mean, I know I don't have the best reputation at school, but I don't think I deserved that."

My blood ran from my face.

"I thought you didn't want to talk about it?"

It took her a few moments to reply. "I just want closure. It was easy when I thought you were just a monster." I cringed. "But you're not. You're disappointingly normal, just wrapped up in the wrong things."

I nodded.

"Brian." I finally admitted out loud. "I wanted his approval so badly. He's what got me where I am. I'm popular. Well, I was. I just wanted to stay on top, and having Brian cinched it. I guess I would have done anything to keep him. But, we never meant for you or anyone to get hurt." I struggled with these words. "When you pulled your phone out, Johnny just got scared. He didn't want you calling the police. We tried to stop—"

"I had already called the police." She looked up at me. Her eyes pleaded with me. Confusion welled up in mine. "I was sitting right there when I heard you guys walking up. I didn't know it was you guys—just kids from my school. I didn't know what to do, so I ran and hid in the woods. People usually aren't out here so late at night, you know? I wasn't trying to confront any strangers in the dark. So I was hiding over there," she pointed through the wall to a spot in the woods. "And then I heard you guys destroying it. Just ripping it apart. My safe haven." Her passion leaked through every word. Although it was just a shed, I knew now it wasn't just a shed to her. It was the way she hid from the reality, for her sanity, back then and still now. She looked at me with eyebrows wrinkled together. I looked at the floor. "I called the police from over there. I had to. You were trespassing and destroying our property. Then I heard *your* voice. 'What are you doing?'" she imitated. My eyes widened in alarm at her memory. "I felt a little relieved, so I came to investigate. I had already called the police." I felt panic; if that was true, then it meant we hurt her for nothing. "When I saw it was just you guys, I was going to call them off, tell them it was just an animal or something. But," she shook her head and her eyes filled with pain. "He jumped at me."

"I know," I said. I didn't want to relive the memory a second time.

She kept shaking her head. "I was going to help you guys, and tell the police not to come. And I got stitches for it. I almost got burned alive."

"I know. I'm sorry." I felt absolutely miserable.

She pulled her knees up and wrapped her arms around her legs, resting her head in between them. Her eyes reflected the pain she held on to since that night.

"I couldn't even crawl away."

This was pure torture to listen to, but I couldn't walk away this time. I sat next to her on the bed, and put my hand on her back. She broke down as my touch turned into a hug, my own arms wrapping around hers, putting my head on her shoulder. I just felt the shudders of her suffering, and listened to her tears. I couldn't do anything else. But she didn't seem to resent my touch. Quite the opposite, she welcomed it as if I wasn't the one that caused her trauma.

After all this time, it seemed like we had spent every day like this. Huddled together, whole. We were just waiting for time to pass. But our patience was running out, and time had no agenda.

WEEK 7

CHAPTER TWENTY-FIVE

Monday. That Monday. Instead of shopping or staying in the room, we decided that the weather was finally warm enough to lay out at her pool. Her mom made us cucumber sandwiches and lemonade. We relaxed, school completely forgotten. Her house was some ways away from traffic, so it was peaceful. Though not quiet. The symphony of the outdoors played, serenading us, begging us to stay forever. Birds sang happily as if convinced their soulmates were near. You could almost hear the hope in the song. The light wind greeted us every so often, making sure to whistle in our ears as it passed. It would have been chilly, but in conjunction with the hot sun it only served to cool us down. It was probably only 65 degrees, but compared to the cold we had just come out of, that was a welcome temperature change. We wore shades to protect our eyes, but not much else. I wore a blue floral-patterned suit, shipped from San Lorenzo Bikinis so that I could enjoy a material softer than most. She wore a pink strapless suit that was loosely tied in the back. She never wore anything revealing at school, probably because of her scars. But in the comfort of her own home, she was free of shame. Eve before the apple. She was so skinny her ribs poked out. I could count them. I stretched and yawned and re-settled back in my chair. I noted how quiet she was.

"What are you thinking about?" A bird tweeted to second my inquiry.

"I don't know. I want to go somewhere."

"For dinner? I've been thinking about that too."

She chuckled. "I meant like a vacation. This pool is fine, but I want to go somewhere tropical."

"Mm, that would be nice," I agreed.

"My parents have a timeshare in Punta Cana, maybe I should plan a trip to go there."

"That's funny because you look like you could be Dominican. Everyone would probably mistake you for a pool girl the entire time you were there." That amused her. "Eventually you would give up correcting people and just start working."

"Okay, maybe not there."

"I mean you can still go, just don't pick up any towels." I watched the water throw the light around. "I want to go to Cancun."

"Where is that?"

"I don't know." I felt a little embarrassed at being exposed. "Or Hawaii." I reneged.

"Hawaii's nice," she said, unenthused. "But so expensive. My cousin just moved to Miami."

"That's in our backyard."

"I know. But she said the beaches are comparable, but way better and cheaper. And it would be a good starting point for our first vacation."

"That's true. I've actually always wanted to go to Miami. Don't know much about it though."

"Have you? We were just talking about it." She pulled out her phone to find a text message. "She said verbatim, 'It has culture, booze, art, and endless nights. What more could you want?'"

"Is your cousin a travel agent?" She laughed.

"She was trying to get me to visit."

"Oh. Well yeah, we should go someday."

"Let's go this summer."

I thought. "This summer?"

"Why not?" she challenged.

I nodded and slowly got excited as I considered it a viable idea. "Okay, let's do it!"

"Really? I'm honestly booking tickets by the end of the week once my mom says yes."

"Yeah," I nodded again. "I'll ask my parents when's a good time to go."

"And we can stay with my cousin. If she's there then it shouldn't be a big deal to the parents if we go, just us."

"That's awesome. I'm excited." I started to fantasize about us in Miami. Charging each other up as we did sometimes. Forcing each other to have fun and leave our comfort zones. Meeting new guys, falling in love, trading them for others within the hour. Then, as if she was in my head she sat up and turned her torso to me.

"Hey, why don't you date Frank?"

"What do you mean?"

"You guys get along really well, and you're always together. He clearly likes you, although he's old enough for it to be creepy."

"Okay, wait," I stopped her. "You're *advocating* us to date?"

She chuckled. "Yes, I'm advocating it. Just haven't wrapped my mind around your friendship yet. But anyway, now that you're over Brian, why don't you go for someone you actually like?"

"Well, Frank and I are just friends. And I'm not looking to fill some void now that Brian's gone. I'm happy with the people I have around me. I'm not in want of anything."

She sat back, dissatisfaction on her face. I cocked my head at her and took my sunglasses off so she could see my eyes. I gave it right back to her.

"Why aren't you with Richard?" I accused. "I don't believe you two have been on a single date yet and I sacrificed a lot to get you two together." No joke.

"I'll have you know that we have."

"Really," I said doubtfully.

"Yes. I ran into him at Starbucks over the weekend, and we ended up sitting down together."

"Okay," I said slowly. "I'm not sure that counts, but yay! How did it go?"

"Horrible. That's why I didn't tell you."

"I'm sure you're overthinking it." She widened her eyes and shook her head at me.

"I don't know what's wrong with me," she said. "I'm just so awkward and nervous, when I'm not thinking I'll be very blunt. Not on purpose. I just can't conjure up the social tact quick enough to improvise, and I never come across well."

"Okay well what happened?"

"Nothing really, we had a conversation about the weather, and he kept making jokes, *that weren't funny*," she emphasized, as if in her defense. "And he would laugh at his own jokes."

"Okay."

I could tell I didn't give her the response she wanted so she continued. "Well anyway, I wasn't laughing, and at one point he asked if I ever laugh. And I said, 'Yeah, when things are funny.'"

I gasped, "Why? That's so mean!"

"I know," she said covering her face. "I wasn't thinking. I just said it. I was just being honest."

"Why? Why couldn't you just pretend laugh? That's Flirting 101."

"I know. He just wasn't funny."

"It's okay, you can make up for it at the dance."

She paused, "I also don't really like—"

"You can make up for it at the dance," I repeated sternly.

I had already wasted too much time on them to hear her say she didn't like him. She could get through one dance. But to lessen the pressure I added, "Even if it's just as friends."

"Okay." A breeze rolled through. The water lapped in the pool. I shifted in my chair and it creaked. "Why don't you take Frank to the dance? As a friend," she mocked me.

"I cannot take Frank to a high school dance."

She laughed as she said, "Why not? If he's going to be unemployed because of you the least you can do is show him a good time."

"Shut up." She continued laughing. "So you'll laugh if *you* make the joke, even if it's not funny." That made her laugh harder to be reminded of her cruelty. I shook my head at her. "What did Richard say after you said that?" She stopped.

"Nothing! He just seemed a little hurt, but then he kept complimenting me saying how pretty I was and how he appreciated my honesty, that it was nice that I wasn't just a pretty bobble head or something like that."

"Really?"

"Right?" she said incredulously. "At that point I was thinking that he is clearly deranged."

"Aww, he likes you!" I squealed and clapped my hands. "The dance is going to be great! We're going to have so much fun." I directed to her, "Don't be an asshole."

"I will try not to be an asshole."

I repeated myself, "Don't be an asshole."

"Fine."

I put my shades back on and sat lower in my chair, letting my body relax as the sun warmed my skin. She went to the edge of the pool and dipped her feet in.

"Hey, Kait," I said to the back of her head.

"Yes?" she called back.

"I'm going to invite him to Miami."

"Absolutely not."

CHAPTER TWENTY-SIX

I didn't bother to knock on the door; I barged right in. She was sitting on her bed with her legs folded, a book on her lap and a pen in her hand. She looked up at me with her light eyes and smiled. I smiled right back at her. I dumped the contents of my backpack all over her and her bed. Thousands of Christmas lights poured out, and clear marbles rolled off the bed and onto the floor. She laughed and picked up some marbles and let them roll off of her hands. They reflected sunlight all over the walls, and showered her face in shine.

"We're done shopping," I said, leaning in to hug her.

She pushed me away and held on to my arm. "Oh no! Did you go today? I'm sorry. I don't remember you telling me to meet you!"

"No, I went by myself," I laughed. I moved her hand away and finished my hug. "I figured I'd give you a break." I moved some of the light bulbs to clear a spot on the bed. "From the start I was kind of bossy, I know that. I just wanted the dance to be perfect. But I know you didn't even want to be involved in the first place, so I got the rest of the stuff after school today on my own."

"Well, that was awfully considerate of you! You've come such a long way! You're all compassionate and humane now. I'm so proud of you," she teased me, leaning forward and pinching my cheeks.

I shook her fingers off and shoved her. We both laid down on the bed, on top of lights and marbles, comfortable in each other's warmth.

"So tell me about it."

"Tell you about what?"

"The decorations. How are you going to light up the gym?" She picked up a marble and held it between her thumb and forefinger, analyzing it.

I thought for a moment. "Nets on the ceiling, like you said." I poked her side. "Holding thousands of light bulbs. Christmas lights draped down the sides of the walls. Silver balloons will cover the floor, and some of them will have lights in them. In the center of the tables will be little jars filled with these clear marbles."

"And little tiny bulbs," she said.

"Yeah." I pictured it in my mind. It was beautiful.

"Hey! Friday after school, I'm going to Shangri-La to pick up my dress. I had it altered. You should come with me. Then we'll come back here and get ready together."

"Oh? I've never heard of that place."

"Yeah, it's not well known. About an hour from here. I like to shop further away; less chance of showing up in the same thing as someone else. We can ride over there together after school."

"Well, I have last period free so I'll be home by then. Just come here when you get back."

"Oh, that's right. Okay, well I'll get there at around 4:00, be back here by 5:30, then we can get ready in time for Richard to pick us up in the limo around 8 o'clock."

Around 8 o'clock that evening, I left and went home. I made myself a grilled cheese sandwich, with mozzarella and avocado. I took it to my room where I ate at my desk. I opened up my laptop and looked for shoes for her. I tried a couple sites, but I still couldn't find anything I liked after two hours. I closed the laptop in defeat. I lay down in bed and decided that Friday would be the day we would have our success. I fell asleep fantasizing about the dance.

◊

Kaitlyn entered into my life five years ago. Since then, there was never a time when it was easy. There was always something between us. My overall feelings for her have shifted from jealousy to pity to disgust, and finally to great love. How do you think that is? How is it possible for one person to be able to fill every single role in your life? For the majority of my time knowing her, I saw her as an obstacle. Someone to knock down so that I could climb up. It had always been her misfortune to have me in her life. I knew that although I tried hard not to think about it. I hoped my friendship and sincerity would be enough to right all of my wrongs.

I did try to apologize before. When she first came back to school after her stay in the hospital. She stayed out of school until her wounds healed and she could take the bandages off. When she came into the dining hall that first day, I was sitting with Brian, of course. He was the only person present that knew. Annette had already switched schools, and I'm not convinced Johnny ever really went there. I realized I was staring at her only after Brian nudged me with his elbow. He saw my distress and told me not to worry about it.

"If she was going to say something, she would have by now," he said. But that wasn't why I was distressed. I was ambitious, not heartless.

I kept watching her. I'm sure others did too; she was a hot topic for a while. Freshman gets set on fire in an abandoned shed. Since no one got the full story—all of us that were there kept our mouths shut, students elaborated on the retelling of it. The best one was that she did it to herself. I watched her just as I did that day in the seventh grade. But this crime was far more egregious.

The second day I decided to speak to her to apologize. Get it off my chest. After lunch, after Brian and I had parted ways, I hung back to wait for her to exit the dining hall. I watched the door as my heart pounded. I had no speech planned, just a simple "I'm sorry." She finally came out the door. And I took a step. And she continued down the hall on the way to her next class. And I continued to stay frozen in place. I was going to follow her, I just couldn't get my feet to move. And then the bell rang and I jumped. She disappeared from view. And I sighed and went to my next class.

But on her third day back, I finally worked up the courage to go to her.

I waited for her in the parking lot. We didn't have cars then, so she would sit and wait for her mom to pick her up. When she finally came out and stood beside the building in wait, I went up to her. I looked around to make sure no one saw.

"Kaitlyn," I said, heart heavy.

She looked at me once, then turned away and didn't say anything.

"Kaitlyn, I'm so sorry. We didn't know that you would even be there." She made no indication that she had heard me. "I understand you must be so angry with us. It was such a stupid thing to do, all of it. I really wish we could take back that night." She still didn't respond. "I'm glad you healed up all right. You look good as new." Nothing. "Would you please talk to me? Or look at me?" I moved to be in front of her face, but her eyes were still so far away it was no use. And then I got angry.

"Fine, don't accept my apology. At least I tried, I could have just said nothing."

Her mom's car pulled up and she started to leave but I grabbed her arm. "Kaitlyn, please."

She finally said something.

"Angela, you are insatiable. You're not sorry, you just want permission to continue to feed your hunger to destroy. I'm not going to give it to you."

The shock of her words caused me to let go of her arm as I dropped mine. She turned and walked to the car her mother was patiently waiting in. That was the last time I or probably anyone else had heard her speak before this year. Would it be cliché to say that she had other wounds that never healed? But she was right; I was insatiable. Because I still wanted her to say the words I wanted to hear.

"Kaitlyn," I called as she continued to walk away. "Kaitlyn!"

◊

CHAPTER TWENTY-SEVEN

My eyes opened to the flood of blue, as they did every morning. I lay in bed for a moment before my alarm went off. I lay on my side, rubbing the interruptions in my right thigh. I sighed and got up, turning off my alarm five minutes before I was supposed to wake up. I stumbled to the bathroom, not putting any effort into walking upright. At the sink, I put my hair up into a messy bun and splashed cool water on my face, rubbing the sand out of my eyes. I rested my right palm on the sink counter as my left hand cleaned and whitened my teeth with the loud electric toothbrush. My hair flopped as my head moved with the motions. After I was finished in the bathroom, I went back to my room and into my closet. I fingered through my options, thinking about what I had to do that day. It was Wednesday, so I had to go to the activities committee meeting. I had a test in AP Biology. I studied a little last night; hopefully that would suffice. I picked out an off-white chiffon shirt with three buttons at the top and a collar. The top quarter was see-through lace, and it had no sleeves. I picked a pair of black leather pants and a black leather jacket to go with it. I came out of the closet in time to meet my mom in my bedroom.

"Kait! Sweetheart, you look adorable."

"Hey, Mom," I said as I packed my bag for school.

"Now this would actually look good with your outfit." She came up next to me and presented me with another little blue box. I just looked at it.

"Just try it on and see if you like it," she pleaded.

When she waited there expectantly like that, I couldn't just throw it on my desk and forget about it. I opened the box to find a silver chain with an old silver coin as a pendant. I took it out of its casing and held it up. My mom took it and came around behind me to put it around my neck. I moved my hair out of the way.

"There. Now you look complete." She smiled at her own ability to pick out nice jewelry.

"Thanks, Mom. I have that activities committee meeting tonight, so I won't be home until later."

"Right," she said, nodding and smiling at the fact that her anti-social, anti-activity daughter had someplace to be after school. "Oh! But remember, your father and I will be gone until Friday, will you sleep over at Angela's so you're not alone?"

"Maybe," I responded.

"All right. Well we will be back in time for me to help you get ready. And take lots of pictures of you guys." She danced a little, excited for me.

"Okay, no problem." I grabbed my bag and we walked together downstairs to the kitchen where I was greeted by a mountain of food placed on the center island.

"What's for breakfast?"

"Whatever your dad didn't finish."

I piled food onto my plate and ate, watching the news that my father had left on. Once I finished, I picked up my backpack and left for school. I paused right outside my front door, looking at the gardenias that flittered in the wind. I wanted to lay down in them. Shed off my skin and lay there like another flower in the dirt. I couldn't stop the spiral that engulfed me again. All of the sudden, I was suffocating on my thoughts, no catalyst was needed. I didn't even realize that I'd slipped right back into the black abyss that told me that I was worthless. That no matter what I did, I was nothing. I remembered years ago trying to explain the hole to parents who didn't understand, and didn't want to. I felt the frustration of talking to therapists I didn't trust. It crept up on me as if I was still on the industrially-patterned couch. I felt myself sinking deeper into my head. Wait. I shook my head clear. I tried to start the climb back out of my head. Can't think about that now; there's no time. Can't deal with it today; I wouldn't know how. I bid the gardenias that I never saw good-bye.

I drove to school in my car, as I did every morning. It was a ten-minute trip, two of which were spent getting out of my property. Once I got there I met Angie on the steps of the front entrance. We discussed class schedules and the meeting after school, and then the five-minute bell rang and we parted ways to head to our own first classes. For me, that was English.

After getting my English book out of my locker, I walked to my classroom. I sat down in my seat, and focused on the window, as I did every morning.

On my way to the next class, I was stopped by Jason Montgomery. I should have known from the line of snickering boys they were going to try to do something as soon as I came down the hall.

"Do you need help?" he asked. I tried to brush past him. He stepped in front of me. "Hey. Let me carry your books for you." I gave him a cold stare. He was the distraction. As I was trying to get past, another boy I didn't see slapped me hard on the behind.

"Look at it jiggle!" They thought that was hilarious. I shoved away from them and continued down the hall embarrassed.

After fourth period, the lunch bell rang, and I made my way to the entrance of the dining hall where Angie stood waiting. We sat for lunch in the corner table, met by the glares of her former friends, my classmates, once again. With Angie, though, I felt at peace. She is part of the reason I have felt unsafe going to school every day for all these years, but the strong relationship we developed over the course of these last couple of weeks became a new form of protection—somewhere that I could gather strength from. She was my light in a world full of darkness. We ate mostly in silence, just comfortable with each other's company. The five-minute bell rang again.

"Ready for your next class?" she asked me.

"Totally." And the sheer sarcasm leaked through my voice.

At the end of the school day I made my way to my locker, the daily ritual complete. I put my books away, leaving the ones I needed for homework to keep in my bag. She put a hand on my shoulder and I jumped a little.

"Angie, you are a wildebeest when you touch people."

She laughed. "I'm sorry you're a sensitive girl. You ready to go decorate?" I could tell how excited she was. I put on a fake smile, "Super, super ready." She weaved her arm under mine and around my waist, and walked with me that way to the gymnasium.

The activities committee was done buying and discussing; today we started setting up for the dance. We would get most of the technical stuff out of the way first—making sure the speakers for the music would work properly, sorting out where everything needed to be plugged in, and getting all of the cords taped to the walls. Then we would put up most of the decorations. Thursday after school we would come in to finish, and Friday no one would be allowed in the gym until the evening when the dance started.

When we entered the gym, the same thing happened whenever we walked into any room together at school. Looks from everyone. Me, pretending not to notice. She stopped at the door to look around. She didn't see the eyes.

"It's going to look so beautiful when we finish," she purred.

She is so dramatic. I pulled her along to go check in with the teacher and see what we had to do. We were each given a roll of gray duct tape and sent to tape up cords to the corners between the walls and the floor so they weren't in the way or too noticeable.

Me and Angie started in the same place and drifted apart. I ended up twenty feet from her when I heard footsteps approaching me.

"You know why we didn't save you that night?" Shocked, I turned to see Brian, fingering a roll of tape himself. I sighed and turned back to my work without answering. I moved down the wall a little. He followed.

"Oh come on. Guess," he ordered.

"No, thank you."

He chuckled. I was squatting to get the cords taped into the corner. He bent down to whisper into my ear. "It wasn't because Annette was easier to save, you know. The world just doesn't need another one of you around. You will never amount to anything. Your parents might be rich now, but the way you people are," he ran a finger down my shoulder. I stiffened. "They won't be for long. And when that happens, you will just be another one, begging for money and food and attention."

I shrugged him off and moved further down the wall, stepping with my right foot and resting my left knee on the ground.

"What are you going to do when you inevitably run out of luck?" His finger slid a couple inches into my pants on my left side and moved around to the front, as he said, "With all those burn marks, you wouldn't make a very good—"

I stood up in panic. I looked down at him where he was still kneeling on the floor and he was looking back at me, grinning from ear to ear. I opened my mouth to say something but couldn't.

"Hey." Angie appeared from across the room, her green eyes on Brian. I was so relieved I reached out to grab her hand. She pulled back from me violently. We both looked startled at each other, and then she seemed to remember something, and mouthed "Sorry," as she grabbed my hand again.

Brian slowly stood up. "Angie, you look nice." His voice turned soft, and I felt a fire build up inside of me.

"Brian," she said as if she just now noticed him. "Thanks. What are you doing here?" she asked, eyes floating between me and him.

"Carol mentioned the committee was starting work on the gym and I offered to pitch in. I came and saw Kaitlyn over here and I thought she could use a little help," he answered. "I guess I was wrong." He motioned at her with the duct tape. "Nice to see you again," he said, then walked away. Angie's eyes followed him.

"Well, that was nice of him," she said.

"You look like you still like him," I said irritably. She looked at me with widened eyes.

"Don't be mad at me," she said. "Two years in a relationship is hard to erase."

I rolled my eyes at her. We both turned back to the wall to tape up more cords.

I got home as the light touched the darkness, where the sun's influence could not reach. I parked in the garage and came around to the front porch. I turned to the sunset and counted out the last couple seconds of light. When the darkness completely engulfed my property, I closed my eyes, breathed in through my mouth, and held it. I thought of the day, thought of what I wanted to be different, and let the breath out through my nose. At the end of each day, I always felt defeated. Perpetually in a state of helplessness. I wanted Angela to see what I saw, open her eyes long enough to see the hand that slapped us in the face every day as it fed us. She wasn't supposed to be my friend; she was their toy, expected to remain docile and malleable. I wondered if she ever felt disrespected. Did she ever realize what she had to do to feel welcomed? Bring your kind down in order to elevate yourself—a crude practice that has become necessity for us. This discussion predated both of us, and made my feelings insignificant. So why think about it? I tilted my head back, and waited for Friday to come.

CHAPTER TWENTY-EIGHT

It was absolutely impossible to sit still through Math class on Friday. I had coffee during lunch to keep myself awake and got terrible jitters. I was literally sitting on my feet to keep them from shaking. Some were writing homework problems on the board and talking about each one with the teacher as the rest of the class filled out a worksheet with questions that covered the whole year's course. This was our usual class routine now that we were preparing for exams. I was so excited to get my dress. I drew pictures of it over and over. Of the dress alone; of me in it; of a tall, dark, and handsome man hanging on my shoulder next to me as I was in it. Richard's hand reached over to my desk and tapped my paper. It startled me and I looked up.

"Obsessed," he mouthed. I rolled my eyes at him. Then I remembered his date, Kaitlyn, and her dress. I looked through my phone at the pictures I had taken of her the weekend before. I found my favorites and sent them to her. Finally, the bell rang. I packed my books up and slung my bag over my shoulder. I was so happy to be on my way. I walked to the door, putting the worksheet, unfinished, on the teacher's desk. Someone touched my hand as I was about to go out. I turned and was immediately engulfed by Richard's steel blue eyes.

"Hey," he said.

"Umm, yes?" I inquired hotly, furrowing my eyebrows. He gave me a shove.

"I got the limo. Black."

"Great. Black?" I had imagined a sleek white limo.

He nodded, "Black. But there's only room for two . . . We'll have to strap you to the roof."

"Great, sounds good. I'll see you later. I'll call you." I started to leave, but I could tell there was something else he wanted to say. His eyes were averted and he was frowning, looking at the floor. Since there was nothing really of interest on the floor, I could guess what was bothering him. I turned back so that I was square with him and put a hand on his shoulder and gave him an awkward starfish.

"She is ecstatic about this dance by the way. I can hardly get her to shut up about you." He looked down with a goofy smile on his face.

It took me ten full minutes to make my way to the car and drive out of the jammed school parking lot, but I was finally on my way. I went straight to Shangri-La, thinking all the way of impossible scenarios at the dance, imagining conversations I would never have. In my mind I would be back on top when everyone saw how fabulous and unattainable I looked at the dance. When I walked through the door, I skipped a little as I headed to the counter to pick up my dress. I again gave the attendant my name and order receipt and she presented it to me to try on one last time. How thrilled I was to see my darling again. It had intricate gold beading in a floral design all around the waist and delicately surrounding the chest as it climbed up the straps. I eagerly put it on and stood on a pedestal in front of the mirrors, while the tailor came and inspected it along with me for shortcomings. I lightly ran my hand down the length of it, over the glittering beads and caressing satin. The ruffles at the bottom made the dress peak up in the front and then fan out in a train in the back. It was a cutaway so the back was out. The dress itself was the color of a coquelicot—the perfect mixture of red, orange, and gold. The dress was beautiful, and it looked beautiful on me.

"All set?" The tailor asked.

"Yes. Thank you."

"You can take it off and pay at the counter."

"Okay, give me one moment." He nodded accommodatingly and walked away, accustomed to customers wanting a moment alone with their clothing.

When I was finished spinning around and looking at myself in the mirror, I grabbed my bag and yanked it open, looking for my phone. I found it in the side zipper and dialed her number. While I waited for her to pick up, I continued to obsess over my dress. She didn't answer. I took a picture of myself and sent it to her.

Perfect. Everything about that night would be perfect. I took it off and brought it to the counter, where the tailor put it safely in a suit bag. I already had the shoes and the jewelry to accompany it in my car, so I would go straight to Kaitlyn's. I looked at my wristwatch, where the tiny ticking constantly reminded me of the passing of time. Only 4:20. I made the final purchase for the tailoring of my dress and draped it over my arm, genuinely thanking him for the work he'd done for me.

She went home after her last period, as she always did. She pulled into the garage and shut the door. She was going to go inside to eat, change out of her school clothes, watch TV, and wait for me to arrive. When she stepped through the door, she would throw her book bag onto the couch and go straight to the kitchen. She would open the refrigerator door and grab a Honeycrisp apple. She'd lean over to rest her elbows on the kitchen counter as she ate it. She had time to kill. The newspaper would be lying on the counter, left there by her father and opened to a peculiar page. The title of the article it was opened to interested her. She would read it. It would make her sad. It was a story that had been told many, many times before. She would flip the page over to see if there was anything else. An extension to the story. A hidden happy ending. Nothing. She'd lay the newspaper back down on the counter as it was. Then she would be done with the apple and throw the core into the trash. She would go upstairs to her bedroom to change clothes and lounge until I rang the doorbell in a couple hours.

But she came home after last period and never left the garage. She sat there in her car, deep in thought. She was distracted, having thoughts that millions from every generation had thought before. Her phone buzzed. She typed in her pass code and the dress showed up on her screen. She read my enthusiastic words.

She looked at the beautiful gems and the black fabric as I did—with longing and wonder. My phone's camera did a good job of catching the light that reflected off the beads and danced in your eyes. You would think that would have brought her back. But it just made her sad, because after everything that had happened, she still felt as if she didn't belong. As if she wasn't worthy of beauty. She couldn't be associated with adjectives like intoxicating or beautiful or even virtuous. The world taught her that those words were too good for her. She was too afraid to even go near them. She put it in the exhaust pipe and got back in the driver's seat, rolling the window as far up as she could. She looked at the picture again, and set the phone back on her lap. She thought of herself in that dress. A hot tear rolled down her cheek. She positioned her foot on the gas pedal. She put her hands on the steering wheel.

She remembered herself screaming that night. And she just sat there. She couldn't make herself move. She wasn't going anywhere anyway. Nothing was changing or progressing. At the end of every day she was still surrounded by the same ignorance and hate that hit her so hard it gave her those scars, running up and down her brown skin. We saved Annette. We did not come back for her. Not because we weren't friends, or because she was odd to us. But because she wasn't important enough. She never would be. And then she fell, all the way through. She simply sat there, going nowhere, and stayed that way as the smoke rose around her.

I came straight from Shangri-La to her house. I parked in the street. I got out of the car with my dress and my bags of products and accessories decorating my arm. I was anxious to show her my dress and do my hair and makeup. I thought about all the things I had to do to get ready for that dance. As I walked up to her front door, I was thinking about which shoes in her extensive collection she would wear. I allowed her to use a pair that was not brand new only because finding a dress took so long. I almost didn't see the smoke coming out from the garage door. There wasn't a lot, but enough to catch my eye. Confused, I walked over to open it and see what was up. I was upset that my worry was taking away from my excitement for the night. All I wanted to do was show her my dress, but I had to tend to this smoke first. I put the code in and the garage door opened. Smoke rushed out and tried to choke me. I started to cough and my eyes started to water. I frantically waved the smoke from my face. I saw that her Volvo was sitting in the garage. Either she or one of her parents must have forgotten and left the engine running. Silliness. Still trying to wave the smoke away, I went around to the driver door to see if I could turn it off. I was going to have to scold whoever did this for being so stupid. I thought of how we would look made up in our dresses. I thought of her face, how her eyes would light up. I reached the door. What was this tube doing here? It was a little foggy but, I could see that something was there, someone, sitting in the midst of all this smoke. I became panicked and yanked the door open. Her head was leaning against the window so, as the door opened, she came out along with it, slinking into my arms as I caught her. My heart fell. I shifted her to one arm and with the other let the dress and bags fall to the floor. I pulled her hair away from her face. She had the same washed out looking brown skin, but there was a darkness around her eyes. My vision became even blurrier from the tears that surged from my eyes. My stomach was churning. My heart wrenched. There were screams. Loud. But unheard. They would never be heard by those who needed to listen.

I called her name over and over. I told her to stop it. I tried to shake her awake. Her head just lolled back unnaturally. I propped it up with my hand and with the other I pressed down on the bottom of her neck in an attempt to check her pulse. No. This couldn't be her. She was alive and well. She was in her room upstairs, waiting for me to get back. It wasn't me screaming, it was someone else. Why should I be screaming when she was fine? I begged her to stop pretending and wake up. Why would she do this? Just abandon everything? She fought for so long, and she just gave up? I thought she was my friend. I thought she was going to be around forever, constantly reminding us of what it was like to carry on with outstanding bravery. No, she couldn't have done this. There was still so much to fight for.

I was on the ground now, holding her. Still sobbing. Still begging. No, please. Wake up, please. No answer. There will never be an answer. I rocked back and forth with her in my arms, hugging her body so close to mine. I stroked her face, still perfect even in death. Someone was there with me suddenly, pulling me away. I screamed and screamed and clutched at her; trying desperately to get them to leave her alone. They were trying to take her away from me, to put her on a stretcher. What the hell was that supposed to do? I wanted her. I wanted to stay with her. They picked her body up and put it on the stretcher and started to walk away. I screamed louder, arms outstretched, for them to stop and let me go and let me hold her still. They just continued holding me back telling me that everything would be all right. It would not. It would never be. They closed the doors on the ambulance and drove away. I fell to my knees and put my face in my hands and let the tears flow. I was done fighting. I had no more strength left in me to fight anyone. I didn't even have the strength to be angry. I was just confused and sad and disheartened. That was my friend. She was my friend. Someone offered to take me to the hospital. I just stared at them. No. I didn't need doctors to tell me what I already knew. I didn't need to see her cold face. I stood up and I ran. I ran so hard. I ran to the back of the house and through the woods and the tree branches whipped my face and arms so bad I began to bleed. I ran to the shed. I grabbed so many dry sticks and leaves and threw them in a pile in the middle of the shed. I took the lighter out of my pocket and set the thing on fire because it was a lie. It would not protect anyone from anything. It would not soften the blows of life. Nothing can keep the world from attacking you, from giving you scars that run up and down your body like prison stripes. On your thighs, on your wrists, on your legs, on your waist, on your back. There is no shield. Nothing can protect you from that.

Some people try to pretend it is not there. That is a lie; it is always there. Some people pretend it is no big deal and it doesn't affect anyone. Some people just don't care. People killed my friend. The world took her away from me. The world could not see that she, too, was human. An insult is hate. And hate cuts like a knife across the fragile heart of a child. I watched the shed burn. I watched the fire get bigger and bigger. I watched the flames dance across the darkening sky as the burning debris floated off into the void. I watched a lie turn into nothing but ashes and dust. I fell to my knees and choked on my heartbreak.

WEEK 8

CHAPTER TWENTY-NINE

I spent the first week of my spring break in my room, tumbling and rolling in grief. Trapped in the confines of my mind. The pain felt physical—everything burned. I would cry and thrash around in suffering. I would lay on my bed or on my floor, lifelessly, for hours. People came in to check on me, but I didn't respond. Didn't acknowledge them. Shadows, unreachable. I ran in circles around my own mind thinking of what I could have done to prevent this. If I had looked closer and heard her words. If I had made her come with me, and hadn't left her alone. All avenues it was too late to take, and impossible to know whether or not they would have worked. Sometimes I was confused, in denial, waiting for her to call and ask where I was. Sometimes I was so angry at her for leaving me. Mostly I was sad. I lost my best friend. Those couple of weeks felt like a lifetime, and now my life felt like it was at a complete halt.

"Angela?" my mom said, her voice pained. I didn't move. "Are you going to come?" I shifted my eyes to look at her. She wore a black skirt and blazer. Her movements were slight and cautious.

"It's not fair," I said, speaking for the first time since I'd found Kaitlyn. Even though she was trying to be strong for me, it made her cry to see her daughter cry.

"I know, baby."

I sighed and took a moment to gather myself. I registered my arms and legs. They were still there. I dragged myself to the edge of the bed. With great agony I sat myself up. Even in my muddled mind, I knew I couldn't miss this day. But the movement and the thought triggered me and I started crying again, immobilized on the edge of the bed. I went to curl back up on my side but my mom slid under me to cradle me.

"It's okay, I know." She cooed. "Take your time." She rubbed my back and held me as I soaked her lap with my tears. I calmed a little, just focused on breathing. I siphoned my strength from her, and sat myself upright again. I lifted myself up on my feet and she helped me put on a dress she picked out. With her aid, I left my room.

The funeral took place outside in a cemetery, on a grassy field. The white chairs were lined up in rows. The reverend had a little pedestal beside the open casket that he would stand on when he spoke. Right now he was shaking hands with some of the people there, speaking to them, giving her family his condolences. Her mom was crying alone in a chair. Thinking she was on her way to do her daughter's hair and take pictures, she came back home and was told that her daughter was in the hospital. I went up to the casket to look at her one last time. Richard was there. I stood beside him and squeezed his hand. Tears fell from his eyes. I looked away from his face and let his hand go. We just stood there looking at her. We didn't say a word. They put the dress we got on her. The gems danced in the sun. Her hair was done in a crown of braids held together with beaded pins. She did look beautiful. Stunning. Too bad she couldn't see it. She was holding flowers in her hands. Carnations. She hated carnations. I took them out of her hands and dropped them on the ground. I replaced them with the roses that I had brought with me. Now she looked perfect.

My emotions swelled back up and I needed a moment alone. I went to the car to compose myself. I used a hand to hold myself up as my insides crumbled. Someone touched my other hand and lightly held it in their own. I looked over my shoulder. I could smell the smoke before it hit my face.

"I'm really sorry for your loss, Angela."

I looked into Matt's eyes. They were a beautiful shade of blue, incredibly bright despite his shady personality. Gingerly, I took the cigarette out of his mouth with my thumb and forefinger. As I did, my finger brushed his upper lip. In the brief skin to skin contact, I felt the scratchy beginnings of a mustache and then his smooth lip. I moved the cigarette out of the way. I had a better view of his eyes now that the smoke wasn't constantly clouding in front of his face. I wondered how those bright eyes that I myself could see through had seen so well through me. His eyes seemed to soften under my lasting gaze. It was the sincerest I had ever seen them. I almost believed them . . . until I remembered. I dropped the cigarette on the ground.

"Smoking is a disgusting habit," I said. I turned and walked away.

There is a bubble around our most superior race. It is one of influence and companionship. It is a beautiful world, one that you would be blessed to be a part of. The people in the bubble enjoy connections and luxuries that outsiders couldn't think up, and that they don't notice. You will want to be in that bubble, and you will do whatever it takes to be in it—to be one of them, and enjoy the same privileges. You'll give them your friendship, your help, yourself. And maybe you'll get close to them, and you'll think without a doubt that you're in. You'll think that they look at you as an equal and accept that you're a part of their world. But in the very back of your mind, you know better. The bubble seems permeable, but it is not. You will never be in that bubble.

The bubble makes them reckless with other lives, because they know that no matter what happens to you, they'll land on their feet, even if it means leaving you flailing. You will learn soon enough that unless you're one of them, you do not belong. You can try to combat this as hard as you want, but you will never be in that bubble. They can be whatever they want to be because they can afford to be; they will always have their bubble for safety. But if you're not one of them, you better work harder to meet them before you're taken seriously. This is their world and they know it, and you should know it too. You will have to give up all of you to keep just a hand in that bubble. I was finally willing to see that, and accept it. I was done offering myself up

I walked back to my place in the flock. I sat down in my seat and stared at the flowers that surrounded the event, letting the tears just flow. I felt an itch and looked down. A mosquito had perched itself on my arm. I watched it crawl over the hairs on my skin. I thought of when she fell out of the car. There was peace in her face. She was finally at rest. I looked around at the faces in the crowd. Tears. Brown skin. Pale skin. Life. All meshed together in a confused knot . . .

I felt like we'd killed her. We made her turn the engine on. We made her keep the garage door shut. We all made her sit there. Paralyzed. Convinced that an ending would finally bring her to happiness. We killed her by allowing the bad things to happen without consequence, over and over again. She thought she was less than she was because of how the world treated her. She would pick apart her brown skin with a mental blade because it was what the world wanted her to do. She let the world into her confidence, and it razed the hell out of her insides, until all that was left was irrational self-loathing and the yearning to be anybody else. It allows the weak and simple-minded to become stronger and stronger without deserving it, while the rest of us allow ourselves to get weaker and weaker. Now, her soul is finally free, but we are still stuck here in a prison of hatred and dominating ignorance.

But no one cares. No one ever even noticed her scars. To them, it was normal. She was just a part of the scenery, along with the rest of us. She was insignificant. She was inconsequential. None of her lacerations were even worth asking about. That year, I was so young. I had yet to experience so much. But in only eight weeks, I had learned true happiness, and true pain.

We just had our ten-year high school reunion, and I managed to go. Mostly out of curiosity. I wanted to see how my alma mater had changed, if it had at all. There were a multitude of events, but I only went to the dinner. I sat next to Carol, who I recently reconnected with. We shared a fabulous meal, reminisced with fellow alumni, and drank merrily together.

Once the dinner turned into a dance event, a boy that I cannot recall ever having a conversation with in high school approached me seemingly out of nowhere. My nose told me it was after many beers that he had the hutzpah to speak with me. He wanted to apologize if he ever made me feel uncomfortable or hurt my feelings in any way while we attended high school. Because he was a changed man, you see, from the experiences he had in college.

He told me that he had joined a fraternity his freshman year. Best years of his life alongside the best brotherhood he could find. All white when he joined. But his last year of college, supposedly, there was an internal vote on whether or not they should let minorities into the fraternity. In the year he told me this, I thought it was incredible that there could be such a thing to have to vote on. But alas, they voted. And the majority favored the minorities. And the minorities were allowed in. And for some reason he made sure to caveat that his vote was 'no,' just to reiterate to me what a changed man he was now. He said in the time after the vote—after the minorities infiltrated his beloved brotherhood, he watched the fraternity grow and thrive. And after actually interacting with and getting to know this man that he was now forced to call a 'fraternity brother,' he realized his error in judgement. He discovered everything he had been told about them, weren't true. What a shock, and betrayal to his livelihood! He never placed blame on his upbringing or the people around him for his mistake, which was mighty big of him. He realized upon graduating college that his prejudices may have blinded him from seeing the truth about the people around him. And ever since, he felt it was his God-given duty to spread awareness of his discovery, so that others could learn as well. And I thought, *Who is this man?*

But I applauded him for his determination and courage to show others the way. And I realized that I, too, had had a discovery only because it was forced upon me. My mind hurdled back, unleashing memories I forgot I had, and would like to forget again.

It all started with a rumor. A stupid rumor that a middle schooler made up. I take full responsibility for that; I should never have opened my mouth out of envy. But they were so eager to spread it. It was like they were just waiting for a reason, fully prepared to topple the reputation of that hard working, loving Black family. Real people. Vilified. I unwittingly started a domino effect that escalated more and more until it was too big to contain. That rumor lasted well into high school, as well as their justification to keep their hatred. Thanks to me.

I was thrust into popularity. Simply by being well-to-do, and scoring the lead basketball player. All I had to do to secure the relationship and my popularity was please him, and share a dark secret with him. Check and check. With her sullied reputation she was an easy target. We started off that night with the simple intent to destroy and ended it almost as murderers. Over my high school years, I gained some good friends, most suffering from the affliction of racism, as was the unspoken culture. It dawned on me a couple years ago that they might not have even realized it.

Finally, senior year. The dance would have been my grand finale. I'd dreamed of it for so long. But alas, I was late to *one meeting*. And suddenly, nothing was the same anymore. At a distance, it was easy to forget the things I had done. But with her close up, she held up a mirror and forced me to re-evaluate everything I held dear. My popularity, my boyfriend, my power. Neither of us wanted to be seen, but we had different approaches to this conundrum. She hid in the shadows, withdrawing from everyone. I stood in front of them, wearing a mask. Misdirection.

In a very short amount of time, I had gained and lost a best friend, learned life lessons, and changed as a person. She stepped in to enrich my life and then bowed out. I thought vainly that our friendship was boosting her confidence, when it was only boosting mine. And she continued to suffer. It took me forever to see that she never needed my boost—I needed hers. And when she could no longer lift us both up, she broke.

I barely made it through my final exams. My friend was dead. And I found her. But we persevere. And I got into a college, did the thing, and graduated. I was able to meet completely new people and make lifelong friends with capacities for love that almost match hers. And I quickly learned that high school is not the end. And I wish so badly that she was still alive to see what more there is. Not a day goes by when I don't think I could have done something better during those two months. When I don't regret spreading that rumor. Or leaving her to die. Both times. If her mother had known that I was out at the shed that night, she would never have welcomed me into her home. Yes, I am as disgusted with myself as you are.

The only reason I had a real, uninhibited conversation with her senior year was because I'd concocted this grand plan to save my reputation after defending her. But I also wanted the satisfaction of knowing that I wasn't evil after all the things I'd done. And she almost gave it to me. Until the chain of events that I started ate away at her mind and caused her to kill herself. Now I have to live with that.

But the riddle I haven't been able to solve is, what makes us different? What made Kaitlyn different? Were her thoughts, desires, and reasons much different from yours? We're all born with the same needs. And then we are raised and warped into products of our upbringing. Why do some get favored and others shunned by society? Who decides who is the bully and who gets bullied? Who decides who we berate and leave to feel worthless? We chose Kaitlyn, but it could have been anyone. We accept this racial hierarchy, but it could be anything.